The Justice

The Justice

Nikhil Khasnabish

BLACK EAGLE BOOKS
Dublin, USA | Bhubaneswar, India

Black Eagle Books
USA address:
7464 Wisdom Lane
Dublin, OH 43016

India address:
E/312, Trident Galaxy, Kalinga Nagar,
Bhubaneswar-751003, Odisha, India

E-mail: info@blackeaglebooks.org
Website: www.blackeaglebooks.org

First International Edition Published by
Black Eagle Books, 2025

THE JUSTICE
by **Nikhil Khasnabish**

Cover & Interior Design: Ezy's Publication

ISBN- 978-1-64560-567-6 (Paperback)

Printed in the United States of America

For my parents:

Nibaran Khasnabish
&
Bina Khasnabish

1

Ime felt the sky touch her head when he told her that he regretted being identified as Udit Saikia's son and that he would've thought himself fortunate if he'd been born to parents living in the slums. Uddipan loudly contradicted his father's views and preferred to do what he thought right, keeping humanity above everything, but his efforts were trifled with. So, being in a fish-and-water sort of relationship nourished by their sincere love for each other, now she realized it wasn't easy at all to break the relationship and walk her way like she'd walked before falling in love with him. As an honest and simple girl, she got perplexed for the first time in her life, visualizing a shade of complexity trampling on her simplicity, a gift of her parents, like honesty. She'd always considered herself in luck. So she couldn't even imagine being out of luck. She knew she'd be out of luck like a fish out of water only if they were forced to walk opposite ways by the circumstances none but Udit Saikia could cause.

Udit Saikia, who worked at State Bank of India went to bank driving his Hyundai, disliked the poor and especially those who belonged to lower caste, considered money above humanity, and forced obedience from others

whenever he thought it necessary for serving his purpose.
Their two-storey building was comprised of twelve rooms.
Six rooms on the ground floor were rented. Uddipan's sister
Unnati didn't bother about anything except her studies. At
leisure she concentrated on Hindi movies. And Uddipan's
mother, Dipti Saikia, was a busy housewife, who had no
time even to talk to the wives of their tenants except on
Sundays, in the afternoon.

Uddipan, the pride of his mother and two sisters,
was handsome and brilliant. The people who knew him
praised his intelligence and integrity in one voice. Ime
had first seen him at Sujan Medhi's residence, where
she'd gone with Papa to attend Julie's birthday. Julie was
one of her friends, and Sujan Medhi's only daughter.
From primary school to college, they had read together.
Sujan Medhi, assistant manager at Jejuna Tea Garden, was
Uddipan's maternal uncle. Under Sujan Medhi, Papa had
worked at Jejuna Tea Garden, and that was before starting
his business as a newspaper distributor and grocer. Not
responding to Uddipan's gestures at the beginning, Ime
had made inquiries about him and when she had learnt
from people, who had known him at Garden Town, that
he was an honest boy, she had carefully made a positive
response, inspiring him to more frequently visit Garden
Town and spend time with her especially at his favourite
rendezvous at the bridge over the river, called the Pahari
Noi. Sometimes he'd sat on the boulders on the riverbank.
Sometimes he'd leaned against the railing of the bridge to
tell her various stories and recite self-composed poems.
Pablo Neruda was one of his most favourite poets. He also
read fiction books. She'd never worried about losing him to
a girl, for she'd convinced herself they'd mutually built love
nests in each other's hearts and he was an honest boy she'd

dreamed of. He was then a student in the department of physics at Gauhati University.

So, after two years of their continuous love, they'd decided to marry and told their parents about their relationship. Though Ime's parents hadn't disagreed, Uddipan's father had disagreed through his loud anger, demonstrating gestures of violence, to make Uddipan get intimidated and leave Ime. But, resolved to marry Ime in any circumstances, Uddipan had challenged his father's authority and hadn't felt ashamed of telling Ime later about his father's antipathy towards their marriage and his subsequent challenge.

Udit Saikia, who had consented to Uddipan's marriage to Ime against his mind under pressure and had forced Papa to fix the wedding date in February, taking the advantage of Papa's financial constraints, had to finally surrender to his wife and brother-in-law, Sujan Medhi, and agree to fix the date on May 26. But Udit Saikia wasn't a man to easily give up. He'd secretly searched for reason to cancel the wedding. He'd also told his confidant that he'd remain absent from home during the wedding.

Not caring his father, who had criticized Ime for nothing and derisively called her *a dancing girl*, Uddipan had inspired her to practise dancing and singing and get prepared to participate in the Bihu Queen Competition. Uddipan's mother and sister were in her favour.

2

With everyone's best wishes except Udit Saikia's, Ime joined the prestigious All Garden Town Bihu Queen Competition, determined to win the trophy for Uddipan. Despite the tough competition, Ime won the trophy, and the Bihu Queen Trophy clamped to her bosom, when she stood in the midst of the crowd of her fans, her best friend Zumur, the first runner up, on her left, they snapped her with their smart phones, and they didn't stop snapping her until she pushed her way through them.

She kissed the trophy, touched it to her forehead, and looked back at the stage she'd never be on as a Bihu Queen Competitor. For consecutive two years, she'd won the trophy. Now her marriage was her priority, not the Bihu Queen Trophy. Not delaying there to let people take more pictures, Ime, with Zumur, walked speedily out of the field where there was the Bihu stage and kissed the trophy again before taking the street towards the auto stand. While walking, not lessening her speed, she remembered her parents. They aspired to see her as a singer, but her first preference was dance and she trained under a guru, for being a classical singer. She learnt country songs from Auntie—she was Gogona Orang, Zumur's Mom. Zumur, who was more interested in dancing than singing, had the build of a dancer. In her absence, Zumur would become the winner. The Bihu Queen Trophy in Zumur's hand would give Ime as much pleasure as it had given Zumur while in Ime's hand.

'Can't you walk more speedily, Zumur? I am so eager to reach home and show the trophy to Mom and Papa.'

'If we walk more speedily, it'll be like sort of running.'

Then, not talking and stopping to waste even a second, once they crossed the bookshop, an auto which came from the direction of the Bihu field slowed down after Ime had raised her hand, and as soon as it stopped, they got in, and the driver, following Ime's direction let her get off in front of their gate, took the fares from her and speeded away with Zumur to let her get off at theirs.

*

Ime's parents waited for her, along with their neighbours. Except the jealous neighbours, who simply kept standing, pursing their lips, shades of jealousy orbiting their faces, almost all of them loudly accepted her as their children's role model and competed to stuff sweets into her mouth after letting their ornate words of congratulations and praise rain on her. She distributed sweets to all of them with equal niceness. She mentally thanked her parents for making such a preparation to celebrate her success, to make the home flood with happiness. She was never second in singing or dancing competitions. But that success was different.

After the departure of the neighbours, Ime went to her room and put the trophy in the showcase. When she gave Uddipan the news that she'd won the trophy and he congratulated her by calling her his sweet queen, she said, 'The trophy is for you. With this trophy in my hand, I'll enter your home in May, as your wife.'

'Thank you. I'm eagerly waiting for that auspicious day.'

Ime went to the bathroom, washed her hands and feet, and sprayed cool water over her eyes by puffing out her cheeks. Though she climbed into bed to relax, she was too excited to stay in bed since Uddipan's smiling face came up whenever she shut her eyes and tried to keep him out of her mind for at least half an hour. Unable to do so, she took the trophy out of the showcase, caressed it, and put it on her pillows, and then, lifting it, she kissed it after pressing it against her bosom. **Ime Borah's Love for Uddipan Saikia**. It was really a symbol of her love for him. She decided to go to the cyber cafe, get this sentence printed, glue it to the trophy, and pass it to him in time, as her honeymoon gift. That'd be another thrilling experience of her life. This trophy would decorate his showcase.

Giving it a kiss, as she was putting it in place, she heard a message ping in her mobile and just putting it in place and shutting the door of the showcase, she didn't delay a minute to read the message from Zumur: *I've uploaded the videos of both you and me. Go to the cyber cafe and view the videos.*

Though Ime had viewed the videos on her mobile, she wasn't satisfied, and she wanted to view them on a computer. Because she had no computer, she couldn't view them unless she went to the cyber cafe, where she used to go to surf the Net and take computer printouts of the papers she needed for her studies. She messaged Zumur back: *Thank you, Zumur. I'll go to the cafe.*

3

The next afternoon, when Ime started for the cafe in the market place around more than two kilometres from their house, it was 3:36 pm. She felt hot in spite of the breeze from the direction of the ancient rain tree. To quickly reach the cafe and to avoid the sun—the sky was clear—she could've taken her bicycle or got in an auto. But she didn't do that because she wanted to talk to the people she expected to meet on her way and enjoy their outpourings of praise. Feeling determined to let the trophy exude the particles of happiness and grow like it had grown since the day it had embellished her hand, she went on walking along the street, humming the tune of a Bihu song to herself. Walking gave her pleasure. Her fans' and neighbours' praise in her memory, once she steered her mind to Uddipan, her mind vibrated with excitement and the picture of the Bihu Competition and the ceremonial presentation of the trophy became vividly alive in her imagination yet again. Stepping into the area, where there were people, she slowly walked and hopefully stopped to talk to her acquaintances, and when none even mentioned the Bihu Competition, she gave reluctant answers to their queries about where she was going, in such a twisted manner that she was sure they were unable to know her real purpose and destination.

As soon as she was in sight of the cafe, she made towards it through the gravelly shortcut, and, careful with every step, walked by the side of the path to avoid the gravel. When her eyes strayed to the rows of garment shops, which had begun from where the cafe was—some of those shops were big; some, small—she thought to buy underwear in her favourite Lady's Corner afterwards.

She entered the cafe. The owner directed her to use the computer in the remote corner, her best place, where she could surf the Net without bothering about peeping people. Too excited to wait for getting the host resolved, she didn't lean back like she did in other days. Her eyes glued to the screen, she was noisily breathing and licking her lips. One minute seemed to be too long for her. The icons appeared on the screen and she clicked on the link to visit YouTube. The server was fast to her pleasure and the programme came up within seconds and being mesmerized and feeling the pride of a Bihu star making her feel like a real queen, as she continued gazing at the screen, an invisible force took her out of the cafe and set her afloat so that she could land at where Uddipan was waiting to embrace her against his wide chest and wet her with the downpour of his kiss and love. She mentally thanked Zumur and decided to ring up Zumur and Uddipan and share the videos with him, just on going home, and share also with Pranati, one of the competitors.

She paid the bill. The delicately rolled print-out of **Ime Borah's Love for Uddipan Saikia** in her left hand, she came out, and not going to Lady's Corner, she took an auto and got off in front of their house. Before stepping into the garden, she looked at the pair of bulbuls sitting on the garden fence. They usually sat on the fence in the morning and in the afternoon, and like she knew them, they also knew her. She went in, glanced at the door of her room. As she glanced at the sweepings on the corner of the veranda, she thought Mom had maybe forgotten to clean the corner which she now must clean before going to the bathroom. Whenever she went out and came in, she used to kiss Uddipan's photo, and not breaking her routine she'd followed since he'd given her the photo, she took it from under her pillows, just entering the room, and kissed it, feeling like dancing with joy, but not dancing. It was the first photo he'd given her as a token of love. She stood by the window. The bulbuls showed their red vents and flew off. After collecting the sweepings and throwing them onto the garbage heap, she went into the kitchen and saw Mom arranging the utensils and kitchen implements on the rack.

'Did you get that printed?'

'The bold print. Do you like it, Mom?'

She took it from her. 'I can't read English. But I can say it looks beautiful. Did you also view the videos on YouTube?'

'It was really interesting to view them on YouTube. I'll one day take you to the cafe, if you don't like to view them on my mobile.'

'Five or six girls were raped at Garden Town and in the garden areas. You shouldn't go to the cyber cafe until the criminals are arrested.' Mom handed her a leaflet from the top of the dresser. 'Read it. The District Commissioner will come to the public meeting. Remain ready to go with us tomorrow.'

Ime had read the leaflet. She had put it on the top of the dresser so her parents could read it. It was scheduled that the DC would make a speech on women's safety, as a chief guest. Six women activists from six parts of the State, including two professors of Garden Town College and the headmaster of Garden Town High School were invited to grace the meeting. The SWS, an acronym of the Save Women Society, which had become a talk at Garden Town overnight, had made an aggressive publicity by distributing leaflets throughout the entire locality.

Now that she was impatient to share the videos with her friends and Uddipan, she thought not to waste her time, listening to Mom and asking Mom whether Mom would cook the climbing fish with mustard seeds paste she was fond of or with some other things. Pouring a glass of water from the jug on the dining table, she drank up the water and left Mom to herself and went to the bathroom.

Coming back to her room, she put the print-out with the trophy in the showcase, took Uddipan's photo from under the pillows, wiped her lips, and kissed it again, her heart aching for him, and then, holding it against the light, when she saw it was as immaculate as before, she put it under the pillows and lifted her phone to simulate a realm of romance while talking to him.

4

Papa, Mom, and Ime arrived at the football field, before the meeting started. The field had been packed with people and it seemed that the entire people of the locality had assembled. Going through the crowd, though she could sit in the chair Zumur and Pranati had saved for her between them, on her request, Papa and Mom, who failed to find empty chairs, finally stood close to the stage Pinto-da, the president of the SWS, was sitting on, facing the TV and newspaper reporters.

Pinto-da's full name was Pinto Das. Ime called him Pinto-da because he was Pranati's elder brother. His father's name was Parag Das; mother's, Jetuka Das. Before her marriage to Mr Das, her surname was Baruah. Out of respect, people called her Mrs Das like they called her husband Mr Das. But Zumur and Ime had the special right to just call her Auntie. Mrs Das had told a small story to Zumur and Ime. It was about how they had become Mr and Mrs Das. According to her story, she once went with her husband to a party at Jejuna Tea Garden. The manager who gave the party introduced her husband and her as Mr and Mrs Das to the guests. Her husband thought that more fashionable and more dignified, and after that they had become just Mr and Mrs Das. Mr Das had got rich from the property of his father-in-law. Mrs Das was the only child of her rich father at Morioni. Mr Das who had once worked as a clerk at a tea garden there had happened to fall in love with the daughter of that rich man. Being in luck, he hadn't looked back since he'd entered the turning point of his life. So the entire property he now boasted of was not his own, though he was a first class PWD contractor.

Most of the speakers praised Pinto-da, thanked him for his venture, and one of the speakers said the SWS message should be spread to every corner of the State to fight the rape menace. They condemned the rapists, suggested taking preventive measures against them, and inspired the people to stand united to support the SWS.

A smile glued to his lips, Pinto-da, in white kurta and pyjamas, stood like a hero, holding the microphone, surveyed the audience with his eyes, and began, '... Now it has become very risky for a young girl at Garden Town to come out alone. At Garden Town, no young girls are now safe. Minor girls and married women are not safe either, let alone young girls. Some predators hunt for girls or women. They are rapists. Around half a dozen girls and women have been their victims. Two young girls were raped and killed after their parents had approached the law enforcing authorities. The police couldn't succeed in their investigations and the criminals had remained unidentified. Lawlessness is reigning over the town and the garden areas in its radius. But who are these rapists? Why can't the police find them out? Is there a nexus between the criminals and the high-ups in administration? Who'll answer these questions? Two years ago the situation was not as fearful as it is at present. Now a lame guy has appeared out of the blue and created panic in the entire locality. We are not sure if he is the kingpin of the crime against women. As we cannot dismiss the possibility, our SWS members have started looking for him. Our SWS is here to safeguard against this danger. We hope we will be able to find him out today or tomorrow and produce him to the law enforcing authorities. He shouldn't be dismissed as an ordinary criminal. If he had not followed us, I would not have thought of him so fearfully. So I would like to ask you all to have a command over fear. I know it is not so easy. Sometimes fear also chases me and gives me the feeling that it will never be in my control. Now, with many efforts, I have successfully built a mental edifice to ward off fear. It has become possible because of the SWS, the Save Women Society ...'

' ... Rape is a great problem in the country. It is also a problem in our State. Now this problem has crept into our locality. This menace has panicked us into making this organization. This organization is a platform to stand united to raise a war cry against the rapists, and to fight for the cause of women. We have set our people to every corner of our locality to watch the movements of outsiders. It is so because we have got information from reliable sources that no local people are involved in this crime. This information has made us think of the problem from a new perspective. What is the new perspective? This vital question automatically comes up. To find an answer to this question, we have directed our focus to the district towns. We cannot dismiss the doubt they come from district towns to rape our girls and then disappear. Why do they do so? Do they do so with some purpose or because of the influence of their genes?'

He stopped and drank two swallows of water. He looked concerned. Sometimes he became emotional. Pranati shifted and inched up to Ime, who craned her neck and saw Papa and Mom looking fixedly at Pinto-da as if they had been influenced by his speech—Papa, who was naturally a non-committal man, didn't look non-committal at the meeting.

Pinto-da searchingly looked about. He drank a little water again. With his handkerchief, he wiped the emotion off his face. Then he began, 'Women must learn martial arts for their self defence. Only writing newspaper articles and books, you cannot do anything. Rapists cannot be controlled by pens. They are sadists. They are perverts. They are criminals. Almost all rape victims have revealed this truth too. I believe most of you read their interviews with interest. Whenever you open a newspaper, you will find at least one report on rape. That worries me. I believe that worries you too. I often try to skip over those pages. You can skip over those pages. But can you...? I cannot sleep if I read those reports. This malady is spreading like an epidemic in our society. So it concerns me. I sympathise with the rape victims. My heart weeps for them. Yes, I fear the rapists. I feel unsafe. I have also a young beautiful sister. You have also young beautiful daughters and sisters. I can feel you also feel unsafe like me. For safety reason you cannot remain confined within. For safety reason your daughters and sisters cannot stay without responding to their various responsibilities. Some of them are students. Some of them are workers. So they must come out. And when they come out, they must feel safe and protected. We are here to help them feel like they like to feel. Our SWS is their security. I hope and I am sure none can dare to touch even your daughters' and sisters' hair as long as we are here. As long as our SWS is here.' He caressed the microphone. 'I saved a girl from the hand of a rapist. I accidentally happened to go past the place, where she had been attacked. As I stopped my car to take a small bush, I suddenly heard the victim's cry for help. The criminals escaped before I could plunge into action. I gave her a lift to her house. They had forcefully lifted her on their bike as she was returning from her master's house. They were wearing masks. They hadn't dropped off any clues. The victim is a poor domestic ...'

After the end of his speech that rocked the meeting — he was the final speaker and spoke like an actor on stage. Ime, Zumur, and others had praised his speeches on the election campaign at their college. He was honoured with *gamochhas* and garlands and was given a Silver Medal and a Citation for his Courage and Humanity. At Garden Town, that was the beginning of honouring a person with a Silver Medal and a Citation for their Courage and Humanity.

After the meeting had ended before dusk, following the president's brief speech extolling its enormous success, Pranati asked Ime to have a look at the news where she was sure the news of the SWS meeting would be published on the first folds of the front pages of the major newspapers, and Ime who was no less enthusiastic than Pranati agreed to Pranati's delight that she'd try to get up early to be the first reader of the news, in their house.

5

The next morning, Ime picked up the *Agradoot* Papa had read and left on the cane centre table under the *kolajam* (syzygium cumini) tree. While skipping over the pages of the paper she found the news about the SWS meeting published on the fifth page. Afroja's name—she was a rape victim—was not published. It was done to save her honour. But Pinto-da's name was published with extra emphasis. He had become a hero overnight. She then read the news in all the papers to know the names of the two rapists Afroja had failed to identify because they were masked. On the basis of her statements, the reporters had indicated that the rapists were outsiders. The positive sign was that the police were searching for the criminals. Reading the front and the second pages, as she went to the third page and her eyes fell on the rape news, she thoroughly read the news, which made her heart weep for the teenage victim and reminded her of Mini.

Mini was also her friend, though junior to her by two years. The friendship between their two families had caused envy in the minds of their acquaintances and friends. When Joseph Huro and Elmina Huro, Mini's parents, had visited them on festive occasions, their jealous neighbours had criticized them. They'd gone to Joseph Uncle's at Christmas. Christmas at their home was a memorable celebration. Guests had come from the district town too. Joseph Uncle and Elmina Auntie had left no stone unturned to entertain the guests. For Joseph Uncle and Sirco-ji, Zumur's Papa, Christmas was the celebration offering them an opportunity to enjoy their freedom. They'd drunk *laopani*, a variety of country liquor, made from fermented rice, and danced without any restrictions. Wine was never allowed on the Christmas day. During the week-long celebration, there was none to control them. For two to three days, Ime and her parents had eaten the cakes Elmina Auntie had given them to bring home.

Ime had spent many sleepless nights, thinking of Mini and her parents. Mini had vanished from Garden Town a week before their house was on fire. Where did she vanish? Was she kidnapped and killed? Like mad her parents had searched for her. Ime's parents along with Zumur's also had assisted them in searching for Mini. But, unfortunately, at the end of the day, they had got nothing but frustration. Despite that they hadn't given up hope, and they'd promised to continue searching to find them. Then, after the fire, her parents had also vanished. The fire and the disappearance of Mini's parents had intensified the mystery. The fire, which wasn't assumed to be an accident but an arson attack, had made Ime wonder like it had made many others wonder if they had also been killed, or if not killed, where they had gone, or what actually had happened to them. Unable to solve the mystery, they'd tried to confirm the possibility of a link between Mini's disappearance and the fire on the ground that the second crime had been committed to destroy the clue to the first one. A girl like Mini with a mind brimful of love for her parents and positive attitude could never even think to remain out of the house, without information, let alone disappearing like that. Mini's disappearance had split Ime's heart apart. Since no complaint had been filed, the criminals had remained scot-free, and none could say if they would remain so forever. The whole family had been shattered into bits to end up in oblivion.

Ime closed her eyes and Mini's house on fire came to her mind.

It was midnight. The month was June. The entire town was asleep. Papa, who had heard people's shouting first, had woken Ime and Mom. They had hurried out to the veranda.

People, both men and women, were running along the street past their house, shouting, 'Fire, fire, a house has caught fire ...'

They'd followed the people towards the bridge over the dry river, crossed the fish market, and then as they'd taken the turn, they'd seen Joseph Uncle's house on fire, started running more speedily than before and within about ten minutes, got to the spot, and saw the fire furiously leaping up. The inhabitants were not visible anywhere around. Papa and Mom and almost all the people who were there had shouted for Joseph Uncle and Elmina Auntie. But no response had come from anywhere, and they'd kept standing, continuing shouting and watching the fire fanned by the blowing wind leap up to lick the leaves of the trees about. Even from a considerable distance, they could feel the heat. The splinters that had shot out had deterred the people from going near. As the fire had finally eaten up everything in the compound and gone down after about more than an hour, they'd searched for Joseph Uncle and Elmina Auntie and, not finding them anywhere, had returned home with the burden of sorrow and failure.

Ime heard her mobile ring and immediately opened her eyes. She ignored the stranger's call, rose to go to the corner of the veranda, where the stale newspapers had been heaped up, and returned to the chair when she found the papers she wanted to read. Papa used to heap up the unsold papers on the small table on that corner to bundle them up and to later send them back to the respective paper agents.

After reading the papers, when she was going to put the papers in place in the corner of the veranda, her eyes happened to go to the clouds gathering in the north-west corner of the sky and reminded her of the last Bordoichila storm in the first week of April and got her to wonder whether another storm like that would occur. That storm was very furious and scared her like anything. A storm always scared her. She returned to the chair. Luckily that storm couldn't badly affect its painted walls of their house. After the engagement ceremony, it was painted for the first time. It was painted in soft yellow. She'd chosen the colour. To trim the borders, she'd picked magenta from several choices. The elegant look of the house delighted them, giving them the feeling of newness. Uddipan had admired her eye for colour and had told she'd be given the responsibility to choose colour when their building would be painted; it'd be painted after the wedding. But their jealous neighbours commented on Papa's income, criticized the colour, and laughed at the condition of the house that, according to them, required repair. Her grandfather—she called him Ata—had built the house with the best timber he'd collected with his best efforts. In her observation, everything was still okay about the house.

Then, unwilling to think of those things anymore, when she went to her room, she saw Papa and Mom making a list of the items for the wedding shopping, sitting together at her table, Mom on the plastic stool and Papa in the chair.

6

Ime's wedding letters, printed in the first week of February, had carried immense happiness to their home, and the month had become memorable in their wedding calendar. The pack of letters was wrapped in golden wrapping paper symmetrically sprinkled with pictures of red roses. Just after Papa had put the pack on the centre table in their sitting room, she'd first opened the pack, and seeing the letters, she'd made sure her dream she'd nourished for two years was finally going to be fulfilled. That was one of her best dreams. However, Mom had admired the letters in golden print and Papa had smiled, feeling proud of his choice. As soon as they'd gone away, she'd called Uddipan and told him about the letters, and her happiness she'd shared with him had doubled when he'd expressed his enthusiasm through his curiosity about the letters.

Ime went out, sat in the cane chair under the *kolajam* tree, and shut her eyes to enjoy recalling her dream of her marriage to Uddipan.

In the dream, two days before the marriage, when Uddipan's mother had visited their house with her relatives, Mom had welcomed them with a pot called *sarai* in one hand and a homemade towel called *gamochha* in the other. In the *sarai* were aniseeds, betel nuts, and betel leaves. His mother had held the same things in her hands, exchanged them with Mom's three times amid wedding songs. Then Mom had given her two silver betel nuts, two silver knives, two packets of turmeric, and pulses. A lamp was lit with the oil his mother had brought. Some rice, a few betel nuts, and a lamp were arranged in a pot called *dunari*. Her hair-parting was touched with a betel nut. Placing a ring on the betel-nut, a little oil was poured on it three times, and then, using the same ring, his mother had put vermilion on her hair-parting. Uddipan had got out of his jasmine-decorated Hyundai. Mom, along with some women, had rushed to welcome him into the flood of ornamental lights and cheerful noises. One of those women had carried a tray with puffed rice, four betel nuts, betel leaves, red, black, white threads, and a pot of water. All the women had lovingly sprayed water on his face. A small mound had been built in the courtyard, with four sticks at the four corners of the mound. In front of the sticks were pots with balls of confection, ground rice, betel nuts, and puffed rice. Placing a pot on the mound, Mom had faced east and kicked it, then taking a little water from a pot in her mouth, sprayed it into Ime's room. Before his cheeks had been daubed with curd, Mom had sprayed water on his face, put a sandalwood layer on his forehead, a garland around his neck, and kissed him on the forehead. Mom had led him to the venue. Ime, who had been led to it later, had circled the sacred fire seven times amid the priest's chanting of mantras for the solemnization of the marriage. Though she was too shy to even raise her head all along, nothing had escaped her notice.

She looked up at the crown of the coconut palms in the glow of the afternoon sun and got up to prepare the hurricane lamps, which were regularly prepared, for power supply was irregular.

7

Before going out in the evening for wedding shopping, Papa and Mom asked Ime to keep the doors and windows shut until their return.

So, obediently shutting the doors and windows, when she went to bed, lay on her back, closed her eyes, and imagined Uddipan lying beside her and trying to explore her virgin body she'd preserved for him, she heard knocks on the door and thought Papa and Mom had perhaps forgotten the shopping list she'd kept on her table. Not going to the table—she'd forever regret doing that blunder—no sooner had she opened the door than two young man wearing stocking masks barged in and gagged her, making her unable to cry for help and put up defence. They quickly tied her hands on her back and dragged her out of the room into their car they'd parked in front of their gate.

From the sounds of gravel and from the humps and turns the car took, she knew they drove her through the gravel road she wasn't allowed to raise her head and see.

After more than half an hour, the car stopped near a forest beside the narrow gravel road through the teak and *sal* forest, towards the district town. A division of the forest began from that bifurcation to end up at the foot of the hills, the abode of cursed souls and witches. The people who wanted to go to the district town on bicycles often used that road for a shortcut. She would've been able to expect a possibility of being noticed, if it'd been daytime. But now that it was evening, there was no such possibility at all, and she felt hopeless and helpless, fear tightening her voice.

They pulled her out of the car and forced her to sit on a patch of grass. They laughed brittle laughs. They untied her hands. They were breathing out wine. She understood their motives. Because she didn't know who they were, she gave them names on the basis of their heights: Tall One and Short One.

When Tall One touched her back and she stood up, trembling, her fearful stare at his masked face, he pushed her to where she'd been made to sit down so that he could sit by her and then, the moment he tried to molest her breasts, she violently slapped his hands away and tried to control her body from trembling. But soon she realized that it was next to impossible and felt so helpless she couldn't help but wonder whether she'd be able to flee from their snare. They were hungry to commit atrocities on her virginity. When his hand came to her back to find the bra clip, she stood up with fury and struggled to retard his violence with her hands, protests, and requests until the last ounces of her strength and defence mechanism failed. Not able to bear the assault on her breasts even her fiancé hadn't touched, she used her teeth and fingernails as weapons into his forearm to make him stop, but he didn't stop to even nurse the bleeding wound. As a consequence of her attack, the beast of his lust rose more aggressively and with its ugly paws, tore off her blouse and pinned her down to his advantage.

Her cries for mercy went unheard. If she'd been in a standing position, she would've kicked him in the groin. If she'd been able to get a chance, she would've broken into a run into the forest. Though she couldn't see the monster's face except his eyes shimmering with passion, she could guess his face was changing colour. Would she be able to stop him? Would she be able to protect her virginity? She turned her head right and left so she could find something to use as a weapon, and though she couldn't find anything as a weapon, she could find an advantage to abruptly force him back and stand up to kick him in the groin he saved by shifting right, and before she could make another attempt, he punched her on her cheek, making her breathless for a few moments.

They dragged her into a house. Above her piercing cries for help, they thrust her down to a cot. They roped her hands, peeled off her clothes, admired her nudity with their obscene fingers, and squeezed her breasts. Too unnerved to do anything, she just wriggled and winced under the impact of their violence. Swallowing hard time and again, she couldn't wet her throat. Fear had already caused her saliva to dry up.

Tall One fondled her pubis, kissed her abdomen, thighs, privates, and bit her nipples. He explored and excavated every part of her body with his riotous fingers and teeth, suffocated her with the turbulence of his body, and let out obscene sounds at the moment of orgasmic climax. Not resting his mouth in the valley of her breasts for more than about thirty seconds, he wiped her privates with his handkerchief and left her to accommodate Short One.

She felt the blood trickle down the way under the wounded area she had now no strength to touch.

Short One released her and Tall One took her again. He used his tyrannous fingers and mouth like before. He sat astride her pelvis, lit a cigarette, and taking drags on it, touched its glowing point in the valley of her breasts again and again. He threw the cigarette away to insert something hard into her so that she was about to lose her senses. Before being completely senseless, she heard them whisper to rape her till she was alive because she was their special victim.

8

Ime woke up to jackals' howls and found herself on a bed of dry straws in a house. It wasn't a proper house. It was sort of a den, partitioned by two over-used blankets. She looked around. Had she been brought to this place by the rapists or by some other people? When she didn't see any one, she looked at the rope burns on her hands, then at her abdominal region, and at every assaulted part of her body, except in the valley of her breasts, which was difficult for her to see. Didn't the cursed souls and the witches see the monsters? Didn't they see her either? They'd raped her very badly. They'd planned to kill her to destroy the proof of their crime. But they hadn't killed her. It was a matter of wonder. She brushed away the tears she couldn't restrain and put on her clothes they'd spread on her. She took a few deep breaths, and, after a minute, she gathered some strength and managed to stand up.

She boldly came out of the house and watched the area within the range of her eyes for the signs of the activities of the people she had reason to be afraid of and focused her attention on the breeze in the trees and the dim moonlight which had added a mysterious look to the hills. Determined to find an escape route, she walked until she saw a glimmer of water in the patches of moonlight through the trees down the gorge, where on the ridge, she stood and again surveyed the area, and then, as she turned to walk right from there and saw a short old man with a sword in his right hand and a hat on his head and his eyes shining bright against his wrinkled profile looking darker in the moonlight interrupted by the sparse foliage appear out of the blue, the fear that had vanished a while ago now returned with more intensity and forced her to keep staring at him, rendering her unable to lift her feet. When a few seconds later, a dark shadow emerged from behind the knot of a bush and vanished into where clumps of bushes had made a small forest and the old man came up to her and fixed his eyes on her face, the sword in his hand parallel to his right thigh, she, getting too perplexed to run and escape, looked down the gorge.

'Where do you want to go?' The old man masked his annoyance with a smile.

'Who are you?' She didn't lift her eyes from his face.

'Follow me into the house.'

'Did you untie my hands?'

'Don't ask questions. Just obey my order.'

'Let me go back home.'

'Don't be afraid of me. I won't harm you. I'm your protector. It's my place. None can harm you here.' He stamped his right foot, brandishing his sword in the air.

Against her mind, she followed him into his house.

*

In the old man's house, Ime got more frightened and perplexed. It seemed that he didn't live in his house alone.

She sat down and rested her head on her hands, horizontally placed on her erect knees. As she closed her eyes, the faces of the rapists sprang to mind. None of them had listened to her beseeching voice. None of them had cared to look at her tied hands she'd tried to fold at her chest to beg for their kindness. They'd just wrought havoc on her virgin body. The rapists should have killed her. It would've been better if they'd killed her. Before being fully senseless, she'd *really* heard them make a plan to rape her until midnight and then kill her and make her a feast of jackals in the hills. They hadn't killed her because they'd perhaps thought she wouldn't be able to survive the impact of their tortures.

The April night felt cold because of the rain and the breeze during the day. Now the whole area, including the hills, was asleep. The noises of the insects occasionally rose above the old man's whispering monologues she failed to understand. Though she was now sure the rapists wouldn't be able to rape her anymore to kill her, she couldn't dismiss the possibility of other problems. Just as she stopped thinking, the thirst and hunger she'd desperately tried to ignore returned. Hesitant to ask the old man to give her water, she lay down to overcome her thirst and hunger. She remembered Garden Town, her parents, and friends, and, impatient to see them at the earliest, she decided to go back home, making the best efforts to the last possible point of her ability, despite being aware of the situation which compelled her to think that it was difficult to nullify the doubt about whether she'd be able to succeed.

She heard the old man stand near her head.

'You must be hungry. I understand. I'll give you food. When you wake up. Now I'll go out.'

Hearing his footsteps, she opened her eyes to a slit

and saw him go out. Averse to lying like that, she came out and when she didn't see him anywhere around, she walked ahead and looked up. The moon was above the hills to the south and the sky was solid with stars. The moon and the stars filled her mind with the urge of freedom and she made way into the cluster of bushes. More clusters began from that point. The twists and turns of the landscape lay in darkness. So, inspired by the advantage from the landscape and faint moonlight, she walked into a deep area, from where new series of denser clusters began. To utilize the advantage, now she began to walk as fast as her legs allowed, and, within ten or twelve minutes, crossed a bend leading to the trees preventing moonlight from filtering in through their foliage. When she failed to move ahead because of the pain, which rose from between her thighs and compelled her to bend double, she sat down to control the pain. After the pain had gone down a little, she rose to her feet and tried to go farther from there, but she couldn't. She got fixed to the ground and became too afraid to even remember the pain the instant she saw the old man crouching under a plant in a bushy contour, his eyes on her.

He stood up, came up to her. 'You can't escape from here. Don't welcome danger. I won't harm you. I'll help you go back to your home safely.' He caught hold of her hand and led her through the tortuous paths and the dips and rises, which were not distinctly visible despite the moonlight.

*

They came into the house. They sat down.

'What's your name? Don't lie to me.'

'Ime Borah.'

'Father's name?'

'Dhiren Borah.'

'Where do you live?'

'At Garden Town.'

'You didn't tell me your mother's name.'

'You didn't want to know her name,' she said with suppressed annoyance and wondered why he needed to know it. 'My mother's name is Riti Borah.' She forgot to look away from his face while thinking that he was an absolutely strange old man.

'Now you are where cursed souls and witches live, Ime. From here people can hardly return. So, don't dare to go out and fall victim to a cursed soul or a witch. At night-time, they move through the hills.' He pointed to the sword, propped up against the wall. 'This is my magical sword. Only this sword can protect you from them.'

'I saw a black shadow emerge from behind a bush.'

'You saw the shadow of a witch.'

'Will she appear again?'

'I'm here. She can't harm you. Believe in me. Believe in the power of my sword.' He grunted. 'Now I'll go out. I'll come back within an hour. Don't move out of this house. The power of my black magic protects this house. Inside, you're free from danger.' He made a boundary with the point of his sword. 'Every evening I do it. The spell continues until dawn. The cursed souls and the witches go back to their places before dawn.'

'I'll obey your order.'

He didn't talk much. His eyes talked. His compact

lips talked. His body talked. And his sword also talked when he brandished it in the air. She lifted her mind from him to think of the witches. He'd lived in the mysterious hills. That wasn't his lie. He didn't look at her face more than twice while going to the next room, where he drank something, and unable to make sure if he'd drunk wine or water, she wondered how old he was, whether seventy or above seventy, or a man his age could be a rapist. As he came out and stood by her in the corner of the small room, she made sure he had drunk water and the fear that had seized hold of his heart evaporated to let her feel the guilt about that she had thought of bad things she should not have thought about him.

After he'd gone out, she sat down and remembered the people, including her parents and friends, who often told stories about the mysterious activities of the mysterious characters in the hills. Though the sceptics tended to dismiss those stories as superstitious rumours, they remained silent when people talked about the special wind that started from the hills with mysterious regularity at midnight to end up on the top of the ancient silk cotton tree at the far end of Jejuna Garden. Let alone common people, even those sceptics didn't dare to go by that tree.

Since she'd been in the hills, she'd only thought of how to escape, determined to act whenever opportunity offered.

9

To avail the opportunity that came all of a sudden, Ime stepped out of the house, violating the old man's order and stood beyond the boundary he'd made, nothing in mind except the thought of an immediate escape. So, before taking the next step, she searchingly looked about to confirm if the old man had gone somewhere or was hiding in a bush. The starry sky offered her a beacon of freedom and she looked towards Garden Town and then walked towards the tree she'd seen the shadow of a witch under. When she heard rustles from the direction of the clubs of the bushes, she hunkered behind a tree, and when after about a minute, she saw the witch appear from behind the bushes and go across the steep rocks beneath the place where she'd hunkered, she got so frightened she wondered if she should go back to the house or follow her escape route. She would've made her way to the escape route unless she'd seen the old man walk out of the deep pocket of the hills, his sword in his hand, turn back, spit, and then start climbing up a rock with the help of the rope, tied to a tree. While climbing, he applied his pivoted strength to move on. In the context of the situation, which wasn't in her favour at all, she finally decided to wait for a better situation, gave up her escape plan for the time being, and returned to his house.

*

When Ime sat down in the house and got that smell assaulting her nose again, she went up to where the smell was coming from, turned and upturned the baskets and the kitchen implements, and then lifted the lid of the basket lying in the remote corner of the room he used as his kitchen. In the basket was a snake. It looked alive, though its neck was broken. It was a big black snake, and was in its coils. What had he done with a snake? Then, as she lifted the lid of the big saucepan, she saw some raw meat in it and came out of the kitchen after making the discovery that the old man hunted deer and jackals, including reptiles. Near the saucepan was a bottle. To take a look at its content, she uncorked it and sickening smells came out to force her to immediately cork and return it to where it was. Sure the oil was made from some animal fat and the old man had gone hunting, she came out to resume her journey to freedom and tried to remove the sickening smells from her olfactory nerves by gulping in the fresh breeze blowing from the north. The urge of leaving that place without wasting even a minute in her mind, she picked up the dry branch lying nearby—it was smooth from use—and closed the door by propping it up before stepping into the area under better light of the moon now above the crests of the hills. In the areas, where the moonlight failed to penetrate, the hills looked deep and green and darkish. She found the star to determine the direction of Garden Town and, careful with every step, started walking, trying to walk as fast as she could, though it was difficult to walk fast, and walking like that, when she stood under a tree at a small plain, the pain suddenly shot through her abdominal region and she sat down, her left hand on her abdomen, and for some time, she kept sitting like that. When the thought that even a single second was precious struck her, she attempted to stand up, her repeated failures making her aware of the intensity of the harm caused to her. Then when she finally managed to stand up and saw the witch appear from behind a bush and go into another one almost within a fraction of a minute, she stopped walking, anxious about whether she'd be able to complete her journey out of the cursed hills. While keeping standing, observing the environment and listening to the insects and the animals and the birds trying to keep the forest awake with their musical and dramatic noises, she heard jackals drown the harmonies of all the noises with their shrill cacophony somewhere in a short distance from her, and looked in the direction of Garden Town before looking up to guess the time from the position of the moon and the stars. It was going to be midnight. Then, resolute to ignore the pain, she climbed down a steep path and watchfully walked ahead, not clear in the head about what she should do now, whether she should look for the old man. But when she realized that his absence was her golden opportunity, she started walking, the pain aggravating her tension. Desperate to escape from the hills before daybreak, she didn't stop despite the difficulty from the unpathliness of the path and from the creepers and plants hindering her movement until she saw a pair of eyes shining about two metres ahead. Not able to know if they were the eyes of a tiger or a jackal or a cat, she hid behind the leafy tree on her right and stared at the pair of eyes, and after the eyes had disappeared in a minute, she emerged from behind the tree and restarted walking. When she stopped to gulp for air and a streak of light suddenly caught her eyes, she became stunned by the streak and sat on her heels, forgetting her tiredness, her escape route, and her problem. She looked about.

In the opposite direction of the light, she walked for more than about twenty minutes. She found herself on the bank of a little river, stepped into it, and while walking through its shallow bed, selecting the areas where there was not any water or less water—it was better to walk along the river bed than through the forest—she remembered she'd failed to see the stars on account of the tendrils and stopped to see the stars, which said she was following the right direction. She neglected the difficulties and didn't care to stop until she arrived at the place, from where she could partially see a wide path by an open area.

Though not sure the path would lead her to Garden Town, she came out of the river, stood on its bank. She looked around to confirm if she was in a right place. She looked down at her salwar. It'd got wet up to her calves. She looked east. She was in a right place.

Trying hard not to bother with the pain, she managed to resume walking along the wide path visibly invisible in the pre-dawn darkness. She walked non-stop until she put her feet on the gravel road, where she stopped to rest for a while to divert the pain. Energized by the thought that she'd be able to reach home at dawn, without being noticed by anyone, she began to walk again, ignoring the increasing pain that she felt was going to seize her hard.

Not long before she had reached the bridge over the dry river, the pain she was afraid of compelled her to collapse to her feet and to lie down.

Cool breeze into her lungs, though she realized after

making two unsuccessful attempts to rise that her body had drained of energy, she didn't stop making attempts, and, on making continuous attempts for a couple of minutes, she somehow sat up and looked towards Jejuna Garden, where the rows of trees were visible like a huge oil painting against the sky about to be light within half an hour. Jejuna Garden was not far from where she was on the bridge over the dry river.

The river wasn't dry before. People of Garden Town and garden areas had fished the river when it had become low after the rains. In its clear water, people had swum and bathed and the dhobis of the town had washed clothes. The live river was the pride of the town. Then over it was a wooden bridge she'd often crossed with her Ata, who had never thought his morning walks complete unless he'd crossed the bridge. Holding on to the railing of the bridge with one hand, as she'd leaned to the river, he'd tightly grasped her hand and answered her questions and told her its biography along with many relevant stories about it. He'd left the world when she was a student of class five. Now that she remembered him there, she missed him, and she'd never missed him like that before. When she remembered the old man in the hills, she intuitively looked about, looked at her hands and at her abdominal region before looking down into the river's dryness, which gave her pain and brought tears to her eyes.

With some efforts, she finally managed to stand up, and then, while trying to walk, she again realized the difficulty, which was due to her long walk from the hills. She took less time to cross the bridge than she'd thought of. She was in a hurry. Would she be able to reach home without being noticed by anyone? Her palpitations increasing, she glanced east, then stepped into the street that ran straight towards the area of the town, and stood, looking ahead: crows were searching for food in front of the small hotel, along with a stray bitch; common mynas and some other birds were seen flying. About twelve metres ahead, there were dhobis' houses on the side of the street and down the street were leafy trees surrounded by hedges. She stopped as she saw a man emerge from behind the trees. He had a pot in his hand. He was wearing a lungi and a white short-sleeve vest. He went towards where the fish market was. Not waiting to watch the man, she began to walk, her head down, and came over to the street that smelled of market. Most of the Bihari people, who were old settlers in the town, lived in the market area, the centre of business. Weekly markets sat on Mondays and Fridays on the sides of the street, and in front of every house were shops. She crossed the market area. She slowed down a little, looked behind, and wondered where that man had gone, who he was, and if he had gone back to where he had come from. She turned left, leaving the makeshift fruit shop and the stationery shop people mainly visited for mobile recharge. They were now closed. She walked by the old Circle Office, the club, and the United Commercial Bank, her head down, her left hand on her lips, and her right hand slowly moving to the rhythm of her speed she failed to increase even with many efforts. Before turning right at the intersection of the four straight streets to hit the street to their home, as she stopped and looked back, she saw a man standing at the end of the opposite street. Was he that man? Was he secretly following her? Who was that man really? One of the rapists? Or someone else? She thought. Since he wasn't far from where she was at the beginning of the street running past their house and she got too scared to even dare to look back again, she turned, quickly crossed the culvert, and walked for a couple of minutes to stand in front of their house. Curious to know if he was still following her, she looked back and saw him standing on the culvert, and then as he looked back again after entering her bijou garden and didn't see him there, she reasoned that he'd perhaps followed her to know the house she entered.

Though she thought to go in unnoticed, she couldn't. Mom, who had seen her, came out almost running, the toothbrush in the left hand, and pulled her into the compound, from the garden. Mom's eyes were full of questions, and her face was bearing the signs of wakefulness, and she looked too upset to speak. Mom firmly stood in front of her and stared into her face. Failing to stand the stare, Ime turned to go to her room. Mom's outspread hand stopped her from going.

'Where did you spend the night?

'Let me take a bath. I'll answer your question later.' Now Ime was too exhausted to answer Mom's questions. To properly answer her questions, she must do some mental homework. She'd got them worried. She felt bad.

10

Ime took a long bath, soaping her body and rubbing its every part with the loofah as long as she didn't become clean. Despite being physically clean, she couldn't feel clean the way she wanted to and it was because of the crime against her virginity, which was difficult to be deleted from her memory. Water dripping from her hair she'd grown out to cover the upper part of her back in a u-cut, she came out.

She entered her room. She shut the door. As she stood in front of the life-size mirror, her eyes went to the marks of bites on her cheeks. The marks on her left cheek were more prominent than those on the right one. To take a thorough look at her body, she took off her maxi and the signs of atrocity on her breasts made her start. Tall One had vertically written LOVE in the valley of her breasts. She closely examined her crotch. The rape had stripped her bare. The rape had left her drained. The rapists would never be pardoned. Upset by the reflection in the mirror, she realized that was the beginning of withdrawing into the world of her captivity, backed away from the mirror, and put on her maxi, not caring to wipe off the tears of anger and sorrow, which were gushing out.

Too weak to keep standing, when she lay down, their tortures occupied her mind and she began to whimper into her pillow. They'd brutally plundered her chastity. Her dignity had been dented. Her mental strength had caved in. She opened her eyes and saw the stains of tears on the pillow. They were not ordinary stains. They were stains of tears. They'd last forever and move around her, like impalpable objects. Their paws which had soiled her body she'd preserved for Uddipan now scratched her mind so deeply that she couldn't but feel lost to the sea waves under the impact of a huge storm and wedged between the fear of being caught and the anger of being unable to do anything. No blame should be imposed on Uddipan, if he was disinclined to even touch her after being apprised of the fact by some sources despite their best efforts to keep it hidden. She put her face in the cups of her hands. Would she be able to live without him? As she heard Papa's angry voice inquiring about if she'd returned, she became afraid and thought it better to keep lying. But, pricked by his subsequent silence that made her curious to know the reason, she finally got out of bed though she felt ashamed of standing in front of them. Before coming out, she examined the marks on her cheeks in the reflection of the mirror—the marks on the left cheek were glaring like a bracket—and arranged her hair to hide the marks, rapidly blinked the eyes to make her tears seep out of their corners, rubbed her eyes with her hands, and hesitantly opened the door.

She stood at the kitchen door. Her parents who were sitting together and speaking something in a low voice stopped speaking and focused their eyes on her face. They looked thoughtful. It would've been better if she had the strength and courage to ask him about whether he'd gone to the police station and tell them the fact. But, weakened by the fear of their reaction that she assumed might go beyond control and result in a riotous scene, she decided to lie to them according to the demand of the situation increasing her tension with its complexities multiplied by various possibilities a rape victim can hardly skip even after executing multiple strategies.

'Why don't you speak, Papa?' Her voice was soft.

'Where did you stay the night?' Anger showed on his face hard.

'Did you go to the police station, Papa?'

'Don't call me Papa. You can't be my daughter. I denounce you as my daughter.' He paused to recover his breath. 'Go and throw your engagement ring in the garbage pit. If the wedding letters hadn't been distributed, I would've burnt them right away.'

Ime couldn't look into his eyes belching out flames she saw for the first time in her life. The eyes made her forget in an instant that he was a non-committal man and not an angry type at all. Because he didn't say if he'd gone to the police station, she thought to know it from Mom.

Mom looked at Papa. 'Are you going to create a scene? I told you to keep cool.'

'I'll keep cool. As cool as ice. I don't know where my daughter stayed the night. So I must keep cool. As cool as ice. She went out without information. So I'll try to keep as cool as ice. And at least act as an intelligent father.'

'Let her first take breakfast and gather the strength to face the volleys of your questions. Her lips have become dry from hunger.' She turned to Ime. 'Don't get angry with your Papa. Don't misunderstand his reaction to your absence. Honestly answer his questions so he can get rid of the anxieties he's suffered since your absence. You're next to his soul.'

Papa threw an angry look at Ime's face and stomped out of the kitchen. Mom put her hand on Ime's back and asked her in a soft voice to tell her where she'd spent the night. Ime knew from Mom that Papa hadn't gone to the police station and that he would've gone there if he hadn't run into Manowarilal, the dhobi, who lived near the fish market. They got their clothes ironed at his laundry. A cold shiver down her spine and no words from her mouth, Ime now made sure that it was Manowarilal who had followed her and told Papa where he'd seen her first and how he'd followed her until she reached home. Mom stopped disturbing Ime with the same question and became busy preparing breakfast, and Ime leaned against the back of the chair and tried to release her mounting tension through deep breaths, but her tension didn't ebb away though she felt a little relieved. She looked out of the window and saw Papa sitting in the cane chair under the *kolajam* tree. To lie to Papa and Mom would be her extreme stupidity. But how would she tell them the truth? She felt like falling into a Catch-22 situation. Those thoughts squirming in her mind, like worms in a bottle, she went out to sit in the chair next to Papa who didn't care to withdraw his blank eyes from the horizon to even glance at her.

Then when she rested her hand on the back of his chair, he sternly looked at her. 'Where did you stay the night?'

'I'm sorry, Papa. I can't tell you about that.' She began to weep. 'Don't be angry with me, Papa. I gave you a lot of anxieties. I'm sorry. I'm really very sorry, Papa.' She wiped her eyes, looked up at the new *kolajam* leaves, and moistened her lips with the tip of her tongue.

'Manowarilal saw you near the fish market.'

She got up. 'Now I don't like to talk.'

He also got up, and as she turned to go, he grasped her hand. 'Why don't you like to talk?'

'Let me go.'

'You can't go without answering my question.'

'I can't answer your question.' She stared into his stare.

'I must say you're purposely hiding something from us.'

'Yes, I'm purposely hiding something from you.'

'You are purposely hiding something from us?' He slapped across her face.

She angrily went out of the scene of violence. Entering her room, she threw herself onto the bed and began to cry, tightly pressing her thighs to suffocate the pain that continually rose from the affected area. After some time, she stopped crying. Papa had never even angrily raised his hand at her, let alone slapping her cheeks. He behaved so harshly because of the anxieties she'd given them. It was maybe because she'd obstinately declined to tell them where she'd spent the night. They believed in her honesty. They knew she was a girl of immaculate character. If he'd known the cause, he wouldn't have violently behaved to her. She couldn't even imagine telling them she'd been raped. But she feared the pain might finally compel her to reveal the fact. Papa had seen the marks on her cheeks. So he had controlled the second slap.

11

For a day, Ime had remained silent and avoided Papa, just glancing at his anger about his face. She'd also talked to Mom less than necessary, thinking that the talk would encourage Mom to go back to those questions, which were extremely hard for her to answer. She stopped thinking when her mobile kept under the pillows came to mind. She took it out, switched it on, and saw there were several missed calls she ignored except those from Uddipan. She thought of Papa and Mom. She would've felt relaxed if Papa's anger had gone down. She'd noticed there were not any traces of anger on Mom's face. In Papa's absence, Mom talked to her though not as freely as before, and Mom never looked away from her face and wanted to know the reason why she wore the scarf though it wasn't winter or so cold. While talking to Mom, she read Mom's eyes and figured Mom's scanning look tried to discover something behind the scarf.

When she stood in front of the mirror, took off the scarf, and the glare of the reflection made the bite marks on her cheeks more prominent, the ordeal came up as live as it'd been on the spot, compelling her to keep staring at the reflection and think if she'd be able to relieve herself of the memory of the ordeal, or if she'd be able to cool her mind and forget the sequences of tortures for more sound sleep she needed most in the context of the present situation. 'Mirror, now you're my best friend. So I'll talk to you whenever I feel like talking. I'll talk to you until I get tired of talking. Now this house is my confinement. Now this compound is my confinement. I can't go out anymore.' She stripped off her maxi and her nudity that was scarred made her start yet again. Feeling upset about the scars, she failed to prevent remorse and anger from occupying her thoughts. She examined her cheeks to find if there were more such marks, and not seeing more such marks, she examined her attractively beautiful breasts she'd proudly taken care of since the beginning of her puberty and touched the area between her thighs. Tears welling up in her eyes, she cursed the rapists, who, not being satisfied by just raping her, had used fingernails to wound her privates. Weakened by the constant pain showing no signs of ebbing, she became unable to decide whether she should tell her parents the story of the atrocities or secretly rot with the pain and stain. Annoyed at standing like that, as she climbed into bed and lay down after slipping into her maxi, the faces of the old man and the witch came to mind, and to keep their faces away from her mind, she looked at the clock on the right wall and wondered why the time was against her. Though keeping looking like that strained her eyes, she didn't look away. But when she heard Mom knock on the door, she looked away and got up to answer the door.

Mom stepped in with a glass of milk. 'Drink it. Your sleepiness will vanish.' She handed her the glass.

When she came to know from Mom that Papa had gone to inquire about her at Zumur's and Pranati's and become more anxious, unable to dismiss the doubt that such inquiries would fling her into the cacti of questions. But no phone calls had come from them, and so she supposed that Papa hadn't made any such inquiries. She decided to go to Zumur's house and verify what Mom had told her in order to relieve her mind from the granules of doubt she would be able to crush only after the visit. But the real anxiety which she was now suffering would never diminish unless she freely discussed her problem with her parents, who were also in the grip of anxiety, and above all, she wouldn't be able to hide the incident forever, and her mental suffering would multiply as long as she'd keep it hidden, though her physical suffering would end someday.

'Women have become more vulnerable nowadays. Anything may happen to a woman anytime when she's out of doors. Nowadays a woman leaves anxieties in the house when she goes out. Especially young girls like you.' Mom went out as soon as she drank up the milk.

It felt uneasy in the room with the closed doors and windows and she got off and stood by the window to enjoy the kiss of the wind and watch the dance of the flowers in her garden. After she'd heard Mom pull the chair under the *kolajam* tree, she went up to the mirror, and angrily scratched her cheeks so the marks became less prominent. But she couldn't succeed the way she wanted. She returned to bed and lay down. No lying position was comfortable except the position with one of her legs on the side pillow. When it became clear to her that lying like that indicated the oncoming state of her life, she felt worry replace her anger and got out of bed to wander into the garden and exchange her smiles with those of the flowers.

For her it was difficult to bend down and caress the

flowers. Failing to straighten the plant that had almost bent double, she realized she must go back to her room, the best place for her at present.

She returned to the room. The pesky pain, caused by her movement, forced her to take the small mirror from her handbag to examine her privates in its reflection. After the examination was temporarily over, she put it near the pillows and lay on her side, her right leg on the side pillow and turned left for comfort—no comfort—and so she got out of bed and looked out through the crevice of the door and saw her parents, engaged in discussing something in a low voice. What were they discussing? She went out. She stood beside them, and Papa went away, and Mom, who was slicing fish, looked up at her face before wrapping the scales and fins in a banana leaf to drop them in the pit near the coconut palms behind the bathroom. As she asked Mom to let her drop the pack in the pit, Mom passed the pack to her, and on dropping the pack in the pit, she looked down and saw the pack settle in its bottom and her future faintly surface from its abyss, above the pack, along with the rapists limping out of it and making the renewed ordeal crawl up like an army of roaches and tiny beads of sweat collect on her forehead, and she felt overpowered, looked up, and dried the beads on her sleeves. Something she couldn't explain scorching her inside, she walked back from the side of the pit to the chair under the *kolajam* tree, where she assumed she'd be able to cool her mind, and just on sitting in the cane chair, she spent not a split second to close her eyes and listen to the chirruping birds in the tree, the freshening breeze soothing her face. Because her mind was still caught up with decision and indecision, she didn't feel comfortable about anything, and though she realized the truth that she wouldn't be able to feel comfortable unless she disgorged the nasty details to her parents, she again decided to first go to Zumur's house to verify if Papa had really inquired about her and then act on the basis of the intelligence output, supplied by Zumur.

She opened her eyes.

12

Arriving at Zumur's, when Ime saw the eastern windows of Zumur's room were open, she guessed Zumur was in, and she entered the room straight off and, not finding Zumur in the room, she looked for her in other rooms before going up to Auntie, who was attentively picking rice, sitting on a flat wooden stool on the veranda. 'Where is Zumur, Auntie?'

'She has gone out.'

'When will she come back?'

'Call her.' Auntie looked into Ime's face.

Was Auntie trying to discover something on her face? To avoid her look, Ime looked up at bunches of green coconuts in the coconut palm.

'Is anything wrong with you, Ime?'

'No. Nothing.' Ime tried to smile.

She came up to Ime, touched her sternum. 'What is this?'

'Have you seen something here?'

'It's a scratch mark. Maybe made by a fingernail or something. Some marks are there on your cheeks too.

It seems that you didn't sleep well. I must say something happened to you.'

'Oh, nothing! Nothing happened to me, Auntie.'

'Did you quarrel with somebody?'

'No.'

'Go in and see for yourself in the mirror.'

Ime went to Zumur's room and faced her reflection in the mirror. The fingernail of one of the rapists had left the mark on her sternum. The marks on her cheeks were from their teeth. Should she tell Zumur the truth? Finding it difficult to keep standing—the pain suddenly began to rise—she slumped down on the edge of the bed, and within a minute, Auntie wandered into the room, the concern still in her stare.

'Did you see the marks, Ime?'

'Oh, that's nothing, Auntie! Don't worry.'

She stood up after Auntie had gone out, and unable to stay inside, being rocked by the turbulence in her mind, when she came out in quest of comfort and happened to stare in the direction of the cursed hills, she felt a sudden urge to take revenge on the criminals flow over her. She would've got some relief if she'd been able to vomit up her internal sufferings to Zumur. But where had she gone? Whose phone was that? Aware of that Zumur's immediate presence beside her was the most urgent necessity at the moment, she called Zumur, and because Zumur didn't receive the call even at two full rings, she thought Zumur was maybe on her bicycle or purposely ignored the call. She decided to keep waiting for Zumur's return, a blazing furnace in mind.

She tried to stay away from Auntie, who tended to shoot questions to know what she wanted to know. Zumur also avoided her when she was in a situation to face her questions. Her questions were not questions. Sometimes they were arrows. Sometimes they were pincers deftly used to prise the exact answers from them. She didn't rest until her discovery.

Walking along the veranda from one end to the other was not enough to please her the way she wanted to be pleased. So, to get a lungful of the easterly, she came down the veranda.

The easterly normally carries dust and compels people to keep the doors and windows of their houses closed until its subsidence. Sometimes it subsides after sundown. Sometimes it continues till midnight. Now the easterly looked washed and in it was not a single dust particle. Thanks to the rain in the night! She wished she had wings to fly like the birds flying playfully for and against the wind. The birds in flight brought her a little respite from the internal sufferings. She heard the gate being opened. She walked ahead. It was Sirco-ji, not Zumur.

Sirco-ji was drunk and breathing out *laopani*. He called *laopani* country liquor and talked only *his* English when he got drunk. He came in, pushing his bicycle. As he put the bag on the veranda, Ime looked in and saw a rabbit spattered with blood, its legs sticking upward. He'd hunted it in the hills or in the garden. She guessed. The sight of the rabbit made her feel sick, and to take a second look at it was impossible.

Hunting was his old habit. At leisure, he went out into the hills or into the forest at the foot of the hills to hunt birds or wild animals. He also hunted deer if he could get a chance.

Zumur and Ime had tried to convince him to be kind to wild birds and animals. But their efforts were useless. Thinking to ask him to tell her why he looked disturbed and unhappy, she went up to him, and he aimed his bow and the metal-tipped arrow at the squirrels in the coconut palms.

'What are you going to do, Sirco-ji?'

'The skurrels. Very wikid. I shoot them. I must teaching lisson to them,' he said, not lowering the bow.

'Don't shoot the arrow, Sirco-ji. Please.' She touched his back to steer his attention from the squirrels. 'Sirco-ji, don't kill the squirrels.'

Displeased, he glanced at her sideways, lowering the bow, and not removing the arrow from the string. 'They eeting small coocoonuts. They eet all. All coocoonuts. Very wikid.'

'See how they're playing.'

'Ther hibit.'

'They're so beautiful.'

'You lik them?'

'I like them. I also like rabbits.'

His face turned pale.

'You shouldn't have killed the rabbit, Sirco-ji. I felt like weeping when I looked in your bag. I feel sorry for it.'

'It is mit you noo very tisty. Lik chikin mit, you noo.'

'When you can eat chicken meat, you shouldn't eat rabbit meat.'

'I'm foond of ribit mit. Go and tolk wid yoor Auntie.' He again aimed the arrow at the squirrels.

Why didn't they go away? She'd talked to Sirco-ji to give them a chance to escape. She held his hand straining the string. 'You can't shoot the arrow in my presence.'

'My irro on de estring. Must rilze it. I rilze it must.'

'Release it at me, Sirco-ji. But not at the squirrels. Please, Sirco-ji!'

'Your looks diffrant. Face looks diffrant face, Ime. Anthing is hippens? Something, something?'

She tried to smile. 'Oh, I'm quite okay, Sirco-ji!'

'Not okay. Not okay. My granti not okay. Something must hippenes aginst you.' He passed the bow and arrow to her. Not looking at them, he came to the veranda. He took the bow and arrow from her. He glanced at the bag. He slackened the string and went in to put it in place.

She came in and sat in Zumur's chair, looking out of the window. She thought of Sirco-ji and Auntie.

Sirco-ji was not a hard-hearted man. He was not arrogant either. Outwardly he looked rough; inwardly he was soft. Picking quarrels with people without any serious reasons was against his nature. But he never hesitated to take action against people if he felt he'd been wronged in an intolerable way. People of his community carried out his command and approached him to settle disputes so that they could stay without going to the administrative authorities for justice. Like the Miller of the Dee, he was a happy-go-lucky sort of man. Zumur was next to his heart. Since Issro-da (Issro Murmu) had won him by playing football, he hadn't thought Issro-da detached from his heart too. He spoke *his* English to Zumur, or Auntie, or Ime to show his power. But he never spoke *his* English to Issro-da. And never in Issro-da's presence either. He'd been Papa's best friend since their boyhood. Papa was instrumental in his marriage to Auntie, the daughter of the Sardar, whose command was considered as law in their community. Theirs was a love marriage. Gogona Orang's family was superior to Sirco Orang's. The ego problems delayed the marriage. Now both the families were in good terms. Since his marriage to Auntie, Sirco Orang had become Sirco-ji. For this honorific attached to his name, Sirco-ji was still thankful to his father-in-law. Sirco-ji had no enemies except the enemy in his inside. It was his anger. When it rose, it assumed voluminous dimensions and he took much time to cool down. Sirco-ji never called Auntie by her fist name Gogona. He called her SDD, acronym of Sardar's Dear Daughter.

The pain was again rising. Sometimes it rose, sometimes it went down.

Auntie wasn't hot-tempered like Sirco-ji. A moderately soft and caring lady, she equally distributed her love to Zumur and Ime. She loved her neighbours' children too like she loved them. She got angry when she felt cheated. She never even thought to cheat people, let alone cheating them. She was a good cook too. Her dry fish preparation was a speciality none could say a single word against. As a cook, she had a position in their community. Her chicken stew was something to be remembered forever too. When community feast was arranged, she was given the main responsibility for cooking. She enjoyed people's admiration and attention. She never ate until the invitees ate. She never objected to anything. She listened to complaints. But she never made any. She was a happy woman distributing her bulky happiness to the members of her family, neighbours, friends, relatives, and acquaintances. She never flinched back from distributing happiness to strangers too. She hardly told a lie. Theirs was a happy family, and their happiness would double when Zumur would be married to Issro-da by the end of the year.

Ime enjoyed their company so much. When she'd be invited to dinner at Sirco-ji's, she'd ask Auntie to cook chicken or dry fish for her, and nothing else. It was her habit.

The pain increased and she got into bed, lay down, and spread her legs so the pain couldn't shoot through her and make her unable to move. While adjusting her head on the pillow, she heard Zumur's voice, and she went out.

'When did you come, Ime?' Zumur smiled at her, leaned her bicycle against the tree, and turned to her, before taking the rolled newspaper from the carrying rack. She dropped the paper on the bench on the veranda.

'After you went out. Where did you go?'

'To Zarina's.'

'Why to Zarina's at this time?'

'She called me.'

'Why did she call you?'

'I'll tell you later.' She stood in front of Ime. 'You look upset, Ime. Anything wrong?'

'I'm fine.' Ime tried to smile like she'd tried to smile while answering Auntie's question.

'You don't look fine. You look upset.' She pulled Ime into her room. 'Where did you go in the night? Do you know how many times I called you?'

'My phone was silent.'

'That's your lame excuse.'

'Did Papa come here in the night?'

'No. But Auntie called me a few times to know if you were with me.'

Ime pulled the chair and sat down. 'What did you tell her?'

'The truth.'

'Now tell her the truth was a lie.'

'How can I do it, Ime?'

'Tell her I got drunk on *laopani*. So you told her a lie. Okay?'

'I'll try. If she calls me and wants to know. But will she believe me?'

'I'll make her believe you.'

'I doubt you can do that.' Zumur bent over Ime and touched her sternum and cheeks. 'What are these marks, Ime? Don't lie to me.'

Ime removed Zumur's fingers off the marks.

'Just a minute. Let me wash up and change into my maxi. I pedalled my bicycle at full speed. My salwar and kameez have got wet from sweat,' Zumur said at one breath and went out with the maxi from the clothes horse.

Should she now tell her everything or ask Zumur to go to their home in the afternoon? When she couldn't tell her parents about it, she must tell Zumur and seek her advice. No hesitation should be made to trust Zumur with the secret. Zumur was one hundred per cent trustworthy. But wouldn't Zumur be too angry to keep the secret? However, she must tell it to Zumur.

Wiping her face on her *gamochha*, Zumur came in, combed her hair, and sat down. 'Ime, we are friends. Aren't we?'

'Is proof needed for it?'

'No.' Zumur's eyes didn't move off Ime's cheeks. 'I think you're hiding something from me.'

'I can tell you something, if you promise to keep it secret.'

'I'll try.'

'You must keep it secret.'

'I'll keep it secret.'

'Promise by touching my head that you'll never reveal this secret without my permission.'

'I promise by touching your head that I'll never reveal this secret without your permission. Okay?' Zumur touched Ime's head.

Ime breathed a deep sigh and licked her lips. 'Last night he made me his victim.'

'Who is he?'

'Uddipan.' Ime blamed the rape on the most innocent young man to secrete her dishonour and felt guilt catch her mind like a leech.

'Where did he make you his victim? And how?' Zumur laughed out loud. 'You became his *victim*? Should you be so upset for that? You're a strange girl indeed.' She pulled her chair close to Ime. 'Tell me how it happened.'

'He came to our house. Mom and Papa were in the market for wedding shopping.'

'What did he do to you?'

'He bit my cheeks.'

'Did he bite your breasts?'

Ime nodded.

'Did he make love to you?' Zumur fixedly looked at Ime's face.

Ime nodded.

'Did he hurt you?'

'Yes.' Ime wiped her tears.

'Didn't you try to stop him?'

'He's a strong man.'

'I suppose you didn't put up so much defence.' Zumur smiled. 'Did he make love to you as long as Uncle and Auntie didn't come back?'

Ime suppressed her anger. 'I'll go home now. Don't tell this to anybody. Not even to Issro-da or Uddipan. Don't break your promise. I trust you most.'

She re-examined the marks on Ime's cheeks. 'I think he was bursting with excitement. Right?'

'Stop, Zumur. Please stop.' Ime stared into Zumur's face. 'I don't wish to hear his name.'

'He's your fiancé.'

'Now he's not my fiancé. I've decided not to marry.'

'I feel you're actually hiding something from me.'

'Don't you trust me, Zumur?'

'I trust you. But ...'

'Just keep that secret.'

'Your secret will remain a secret forever. Like a precious treasure. Don't worry.'

'Now let me go.'

'Ime, I advise you to call Uddipan and talk to him to repair the relationship.'

'I'll never call him. I'll never talk to him.'

'Never?'

'Yes. Never.'

'Why?'

'I'll never marry.'

'Is it your final decision?'

'Yes, it is my final decision.'

'Alter your decision.'

'I will never alter my decision.'

'If you don't alter your decision, I'll cut my friendship with you.'

'It's your promise?'

'Yes. It is my promise. I promise by touching your head.'

'It's a hard promise, Zumur.'

'I understand.'

'Alter this hard promise if you really understand.'

'I will never alter my promise if you don't alter your decision.'

'I'll hug you before I say goodbye to you forever.'

'Do you know what you're really talking about?' Zumur asked, not looking away from Ime's face.

'I'm cool.'

'Aren't you afraid of being a loser?'

'I'm already a loser.'

'I ask you to alter your decision for your own good, Ime. Don't be so headstrong. Don't be so hot-headed.'

'I'll never alter my decision.'

'Won't you even remember me?'

'No.'

Ime came out and looked at Sirco-ji sitting on the veranda, the bow about a foot away from his feet near the bag with the rabbit in it. He had put his arrows in the sheath. She knelt down. Her right knee touched the strained string. She asked him to stop hunting wild animals and birds.

Zumur walked up to them, lifted the bag, and looked in and took the rabbit out of the bag, by its leg, and keeping staring at its open eyes, she touched the stains of its tears, then held it in front of him.

Sirco-ji looked up at her face. 'What this dramacting, Zumur?'

'Again you've hunted a rabbit, Papa? Didn't I ask you not to hunt wild animals and birds? What will you do with it? Will you eat its meat? Who'll cook its meat for you? Mom? Or you yourself? Look at it. Do you know what it is? It is not a rabbit. It is *me*. It is your daughter.' Unable to check her tears, she heavily sat on the floor of the veranda, the rabbit in her hand. 'Yes, it's me. It is me, Papa!'

'Kul dwn, kul dwn, Beeti. Me not killing willd

onimols or birds future time never. Okay? My promiss.' He pinched his Adam's apple.

'Remember I'm your daughter. You kill a wild animal or a bird. Means you kill me.'

'Oh, no speek lik that, Beeti!' He hugged her into his chest. He became emotional. He kissed her time and again, fondling her head with his chin. Then he looked at Ime. 'You teking dinner here widus, Ime.'

'I'll cook dry fish and chicken for you,' Auntie said from behind.

'Thank you. Not today. Some other day.'

'My irros not target missing, Ime. Just weiting find the ripists out. They can't doo anthing. Don't feer them. Pinto widus. SWS widus.'

Ime nodded to please him. Then, before she came out, Auntie hugged her and lovingly smoothed her cheeks with her hand. Zumur was looking at them.

'Bye, Zumur.'

'If you don't alter your decision, remember my promise.'

'Okay.'

Ime felt as though she was the rabbit. She closed the gate. Determined not to look back, she speedily walked to take the turn to disappear from their sight.

After taking the turn, she took an auto for her home.

13

Ime had felt extremely disgruntled at the way Zumur had reacted to what she had told Zumur, and on account of that—another reason was the severity of the pain, which needed urgent medical treatment—she had a difficult sleep in the night despite she had resolved to have a sound sleep and had gone to bed early. So, with the decision to tell Mom the truth, when she got up, she didn't care to arrange her hair to hide the marks.

She went to the kitchen and sat in the chair at the dining table, and Mom, who was busy preparing breakfast, came up to her, looked into her face, and examined the marks with her fingers, curious to know the reason. But, Ime, not satisfying Mom's curiosity, went away to the toilet, after drinking two glasses of warm water she used to drink.

As Ime came back and sat at the dining table to eat breakfast, Papa, who had stopped talking to her since he had slapped on her cheek, peeped in and went away, giving her the impression that he disliked sitting with her at the same table.

Mom brought a bunch of ripe banana from the storeroom. 'Where's your Papa?'

'Don't know.'

'Didn't he talk to you?'

'No.'

'Didn't you talk to him?'

'I'll never talk to him.'

While eating rice flakes with milk, her attention flitting between her bowl and Mom's inquisitive eyes, she tried to remain collected, though how-she-should-begin was blowing in her mind, like a storm. She was their beautiful daughter, their pride, their dream, and the fountain of their happiness. Now, not caring about those things and whether Mom would be able to bear the brunt of the blow, she decided to reveal the fact to Mom. She looked up when Mom dropped two peeled bananas into her bowl.

After finishing eating, she stood up to go to the basin and the pain suddenly woke up and she bent double and sat down, her head on her interlocked hands on the table and Mom immediately came up to her and put her hand on her head, anxious to know the reason why she'd bent double like that, and not telling Mom the reason, she allowed about five minutes to pass in silence to fight the pain before going to the basin. She took more than usual time to wash her hands and rinse her mouth so that she could collect the courage and find appropriate words to deliver the details of her pain to Mom. Returning to the chair — the pain had also made her bold — she licked her lips, breathed a deep sigh, and then pointed her left forefinger to the marks. 'Now I'm going to tell you something very important, Mom. You must keep it secret from Papa.'

'I'll keep it secret.'

When Ime finished telling Mom about the incident, Mom slumped to her knees and started beating her head against the leg of the chair she had sat in. She helped Mom to her feet, made her sit in the chair, and wiped her tears.

'I curse the rapists. A thunderbolt will kill them. A storm will kill them. A sudden fire will burn their houses and kill them. Their whole families will be destroyed. Their generations will be destroyed. I curse them. Bleeding like a butchered animal, they'll breathe their last.' Mom laid her head on the table and began to cry again. 'They raped you ahead of your wedding. Now what'll be about your wedding? Oh God, why don't you take me away from this world? Why am I still living? God, take me away from this world.'

She'd never seen Mom get so angry. She'd never heard Mom curse anyone. She let Mom cry at the pitch of her voice dripping venom and waited for her to stop crying.

A couple of minutes later, Mom raised her head and stared at her cheeks. 'We are parents. Only a raped daughter's parents can feel the depth of the wound their daughter suffers.'

Sure Mom would talk more, it was her habit to talk on and on until her mind became empty of words of advice, Ime turned away to quickly find herself in her room she had thought her confinement since her escape from the hills.

The constantly intolerable pain constrained her to examine her inside. It had become clammy. She decided to receive urgent medical treatment. But what was the guarantee that the treatment would be kept secret? She called out to Mom to come to her room so she could discuss the complexity of the condition.

Mom came in and listened to her problem.

'Don't worry. I'll leave no stone unturned to help you.'

14

The next afternoon, Mom brought medicine for Ime from Burha Bej's wife, who lived in their cottage near Jejuna Garden and practised herbal medicine, and assured Ime that the medicine would cure her and that Burha Bej's wife believed Mom's lies and would keep it secret.

Some herbs had been pasted; some herbs had been crushed into balls. Not allowing Mom to interfere with how to use the medicine, she applied it to her cheeks and bosom. Before applying it between her thighs, she lay on her back and continued lying like that until its bite lessened.

Though she didn't feel as cool as desired, she got up, hearing the sound of Papa's bicycle, and tried to listen if Mom charged Papa with slapping her or talked to him to reveal the fact. But she didn't hear them speak. She only heard sounds of the kitchen implements Mom was using for cooking dinner. She hadn't cooked at noon because of being at Burha Bej's. Since her returning home from the hills, he had become reticent and talked to Mom only out of necessity. Why wasn't he now driven by necessity to ask Mom why she was cooking late in contrast to her routine she'd followed without a break?

Not going back to her bed, she stood in front of the life-size mirror to study her face. She either talked to her reflection or studied her face in the mirror whenever she felt upset or afraid.

15

Ime's parents, who barely quarrelled or argued with each other, had often quarrelled and argued with each other since her return from the cursed hills. Ime heard them loudly quarrel about something—Mom's voice was above Papa's—and assumed that none of them was in a mood to stop, and so, to know the cause for the quarrel, she listened at the closed door of the room they were in.

'Why did you slap my daughter? What made you turn into a tyrant?' Mom roared.

'A tyrant? I've become a tyrant? Have you forgotten she's wearing the engagement ring? Where did she actually spend the night? Manowarilal saw her come from the direction of the bridge. Why can't she tell where she spent the night? And you call me a tyrant and stand by your daughter?'

'She is not your daughter?'

'No. She is not my daughter anymore.'

'You are not just a beast. You are a mad beast.'

'Now I'll show I'm a real beast.'

On hearing loud thumps, Ime didn't waste a

second to throw the door open and grasp the flat piece of wood to prevent Papa from striking Mom on her back. The piece was used for blocking the gap under the threshold. The piece in her hand, she boldly faced him. 'What has happened to you, Papa? Why have you beaten Mom? What's her guilt? She's not guilty. I am guilty. I stayed the night outside. But Mom didn't. So what's her guilt?'

'You have become so courageous, Ime,' he said through gritted teeth.

'Yes, I have become so courageous. What'll you do now? Will you beat me? Beat me if you can. I am ready to receive your violence. Break it on my back. Break it.' Ime thrust the piece into his hand. 'Why are you standing? Break it on my back.'

He threw the piece out through the door and went out, and Mom, who had howled, splitting the roofs of the house, now whimpered and cursed her fate before falling silent. Ime touched Mom's back, and Mom sat up and, with tearful eyes, looked at Ime's tear-sodden cheeks.

'Has he gone mad, Mom? I never saw him even harshly behave to you, let alone striking you with something. This sudden change in his behaviour indicates something we should be careful about. Mom, never argue with him. Keep him under observation.'

'I can't forgive him. He didn't let us get prepared to tell him the truth.'

Mom got out of bed, and Papa stepped into the room. He still looked angry, and from his look, it was apparent that the storm that had started blowing in his mind since that night would subside only after the truth was revealed to him. What should she do? Should she tell him the truth like she'd told Mom?

'You can't forgive me! Have I sought your forgiveness? What'll happen to me if you don't forgive me? Do I care about your forgiveness?' Papa flexed his muscles.

'You shouldn't forget only a few days are ahead of the wedding. Give me any punishment after the wedding. Now control your temper,' Mom said, a tone of anger in her voice.

'Who will marry your daughter? Who will marry a girl like your daughter? Do you think Manowarilal will keep mum? Do you think Garden Town won't know your daughter returned home at dawn, spending night elsewhere? She's *your* daughter. So do whatever you think the best.' He thumped the door and stormed from the room.

Finding it impossible to stand the blow of his vitriolic words, Ime rushed up to Mom's wardrobe, opened it, and took out the wedding clothes they'd bought that fateful evening.

'Why have you taken them out, Ime? What do you want to do with them?' Mom asked.

'I'll keep them in my wardrobe. Let me go.' She came out, lowering her head, the clothes clutched to her bosom.

Her bleak future wrenching at her heart, she put them down on her reading table, found herself in the cane chair under the *kolajam* tree, and looked up at the crown of the coconut palms in the glow of the afternoon sun.

16

In the afternoon, the next day, Ime's eyes happened to go to the clouds gathering in the north-west corner of the sky, and she remembered the last Bordoichila storm in the first week of April and wondered another storm like that might occur. A storm scared her. Though that storm was very furious and scared her like anything, it couldn't badly affect the painted walls of their house. That was their good luck.

After the engagement ceremony, their house, which was painted for the first time, was painted in soft yellow. She'd chosen the colour. To trim the borders, she'd picked magenta from several choices. The elegant look of the house delighted them, giving them the feeling of newness. Their jealous neighbours commented on Papa's income, criticized the colour, and laughed at the condition of the house that, according to them, required repair. But, in her observation, everything was still okay about the house. Ata had built the house with the best timber he'd collected with his best efforts.

*

In the night, Ime woke up to the huge noises of the

crushing storm and hail on the corrugated tin roof of her room, and except the noises of the storm and hail and the flashes of lightning through the sash windows and the crevices, nothing could be heard and seen. The power failure worsened the situation. She sat up and gathered her mattress when the storm raging over the entire town or maybe the entire garden area drove rainwater and small hail into the room. Feeling sorry for the poor garden workers and their small huts which hadn't been adequately built to bear the brunt of such a fierce storm, she got off and tried to see the outside, though she couldn't open the window, and when she could see nothing except darkness, split by lightning, she came back to bed and thought it wouldn't subside before long, for it was the heaviest storm of the year and even more forceful and furious than the Bordoichila of April. Uneasy about sitting on the bed, she got off again and started pacing down the floor, her mind packed with concern. Failing to talk to her parents, who had kept their mobiles switched off, and to Zumur, who didn't receive her calls, she stood at the door so he could open it and go out if the house failed to repel the violence of the storm. She was more afraid of being smothered than being hit by the storm and rain and hail. The frequency of thunder and lightning forced her to climb into bed and lean back against its headboard, watching the outside through the sash windows and listening to the staccato music of the intermittent hail and continuous downpour. As she closed her eyes after having a glimpse at the sash window lit by the flash of lightning and heard Papa knocking hard at the door and calling out to her, she read the time on her mobile—it was 2:16 am—got off, went to the veranda in no time, and saw rainwater flowing down the courtyard to meet the drain.

'Where's your Mom?'

'Wasn't she in your room?'

'She was. But now she's not in my room.'

Though the hail had stopped falling and the downpour had lessened a little, lightning was still being followed by crashing thunder like before and they could see the objects only when lightning split the darkness embracing the objects into its enormous bosom. Searchingly looking around from where they were on the veranda, they loudly called out to Mom. But no response came from her. Anxieties grating on their hearts, when they decided to keep standing on the veranda until the abatement of the downpour, Ime suddenly happened to see in the flash of lightning an object like a human in a sedentary position at the foot of the *kolajam* tree, grasped Papa's hand, pulled him down the veranda into the flowing flood, and walked through the downpour up to the foot of the tree. It was Mom, who was sitting there, leaning her head against the trunk, unmindful of the downpour. Hadn't hail hit her?

'What are you doing here, Mom? Why have you come here? *Why*?' Ime tried to help her to her feet, with the help of Papa. Ime sat down, embraced Mom, and made unsuccessful attempts to lift her.

Papa gripped Mom's hands to pull her to stand up, and Mom, adamant not to stand up, wrenched her hands free and shifted left.

'Let more hail beat me. Let the rain wash away my sorrows. Let the lightning strike me hard. The hail couldn't beat me down to earth. The rain couldn't wash away my sorrows. No lightning struck me to take the life out of me. I won't go inside. You can't take me inside. Now I'm waiting for the fatal lightning.' She was shivering with cold.

After they'd forcibly dragged her into Ime's room, Ime lit the lamp and Papa seated her on the chair. Mom wore dry clothes Papa had got her. They went back to their room. Ime continued standing, keeping the door open and listening to the rumble of thunder and watching the darkness, sliced by the lightning and the downpour flooding the courtyard. On an impulse, she turned from the door, picked up the wedding clothes from the table, went out to the corner of the veranda, and furiously threw them into the running rainwater so that they were carried into the drain flowing like a little river. Not looking at the clothes more than twice, she came in, changed into her maxi, and went to bed to wait for the dawn.

The pain hadn't stopped disturbing her, though the area was healing.

17

Sure the wedding clothes had gone to the drain, Ime came out and stood down the veranda, after looking at the rising sun. When she saw the hailstorm, which had heavily blown over the entire town, had broken two big branches of the *kolajam* tree and blown them away to the front of the outhouse beside the rows of mango and jackfruit trees, she went ahead and saw the storm had affected the mud-plastered walls and the plasters had peeled off. The walls were built with thatch. As the garden came to mind, she wandered into the garden and shuddered at the damage, caused by the hail and downpour. The plants had been stripped of leaves and flowers. She must ignore the pain and labour hard for the garden, and that hard labour would help her forget her marriage. But when she wondered if she could forget the distributed wedding letters and if Papa could visit every house to tell the invitees that the marriage had been cancelled, she felt a thunderbolt hit her head. Her parents were still unaware of her decision that she wouldn't marry, and after she'd made the decision, which was the hardest one she'd made against her mind, she ignored Uddipan's calls, determined not to even talk to him in case he came to meet her. She would've thrown the letters into the murmuring drain if they'd been in the house at the moment.

'The rain tree has damaged our grocery shop too,' Papa said. 'It was difficult for me to stand the sight.'

'Now the family will have to struggle hard to satisfy hunger,' Mom said while wiping her tearful eyes.

'Papa, let's go to see the tree.'

*

The rain tree had stood for more than a hundred years to the west of Garden Town English School as the pride of Garden Town. The tree had been revengefully broken by the storm, which had perhaps more violently blown over that area than over the other ones. As her look went to their small shop lying crushed under the tree—in the afternoon, Papa used to sit in that shop for some extra money after distributing paper—she felt numbness come down on her and couldn't decide if she should lean against Papa or slump down, unable to look away from the shop and the tree blocking the road crosswise and making her remember how its branches had interlocked to make solid shade that the sun could hardly penetrate. In its shade, people relaxed. In its shade were small shops like Papa's on the roadside slanting towards the pond about a hundred metres away. The shops built on high posts looked like hoisted structures from the other side of the pond. Except one shop that was now sadly standing out beyond the width of the trunk and mutilated branches of the tree, all the shops under the tree had been damaged. They belonged to poor people like them. Some goods had been recovered; some goods had remained barricaded by the branches. Unless the tree was butchered out and removed, it'd be difficult to recover the goods.

Extremely disappointed at the condition of the tree and crushed shops, Ime touched Papa's back and Papa glanced at her over his right shoulder. She indicated with her brows to leave for home. She also felt the need to apply the medicine.

*

As soon as she entered her room, the phone rang, and she answered Pranati's call. After discussing the hail and rain, Pranati told her that Pinto-da, who had gone to Guwahati with Innes-bhai, had given them tension, not receiving their phone calls, and ignoring their messages.

'Do you suspect Innes-bhai?' Ime asked.

'Innes-bhai is not only his driver, but also his friend.'

'Scorpio is an expensive car. In such cases people normally tend to suspect the driver.'

'But we don't suspect Innes-bhai.'

'Did your Papa go to the police station?'

'We'll wait for another week. Then we'll do what we think the best.'

'Do you think it's a case of kidnapping?'

'None has still demanded ransom money. So we can't say it's a case of kidnapping.'

'Now it's time to pray for their safe return.'

'Right. But ... Ime, don't tell anyone about it.'

'Okay.'

Ime went to bed and before applying the medicine, she prayed for their safe return. Pleased with the effect of the medicine, she kept lying as she'd kept lying before. The medicine was rapidly healing her external wound. But it couldn't heal her mental suffering, which was increasing as the wedding day was approaching. It was easy to get rid of the wedding clothes, but not easy to get rid of the wedding date. Now it was high time to tell the invitees and relatives about the cancellation of the wedding. Wouldn't they demand the cause for the cancellation? Would Papa be able to say that the wedding had been cancelled because his daughter had been raped? If a storm came now, she would jump out of bed and ran to the field to receive lightning she now thought to be her best relief.

Feeling as though she were Sirco-ji's rabbit or their crushed shop under the rain tree, she got out of bed, and emerged to summon up the energy by breathing in fresh air so she could stand the suffering, which was going to erode the power of her endurance. A small cool breeze stroking her face, she sat in the cane chair under the *kolajam* tree and looked up and around. Now no birds were in the tree. Parts of torn leaves Mom couldn't sweep away were lying stuck to the earth, softened by the rain. Small insects were flying about. Papa coughed aloud and she turned her head left and saw him come out of the kitchen garden with vegetables in a basket.

Uddipan messaged her. Though she hesitated to open the message, she couldn't help but do it:

You don't receive my calls. You don't call me. If you don't answer this message, I'll believe you think me a lout, not a fiancé. And I'll neither call you nor send you a message. Nor a poem either. Now read my LOVE. Through LOVE, I've told what I wanted to tell you. Read LOVE whenever you remember me. It'll silently talk to you. Your loving fiancé.

LOVE

What you do not speak is really spoken.

A poet's mind's sharp ears can listen

to what is left unspoken.

Love is not love that does not lie in love.

Love is love that tends to seek love's hide-out,

and only a lover knows love, but never a lout.

Tears dropped on fiancé and rolled to *LOVE*.

Papa came up to her. 'What're you doing, Ime?'

'Nothing.' She hurriedly wiped her eyes.

'I don't know.' He sat down. 'I think your Mom is trying to hide something from me.'

'I couldn't sleep well in the night. I feel sleepy.'

'May I know why you threw the wedding clothes into the rainwater? I collected the clothes from the garden. They were sticking to the garden fence.' He didn't lower his look fixed on her face. 'You are my sweet daughter, Ime. Don't be afraid of anything. Just tell me the truth.'

'I've decided not to marry.'

He sprang up from the chair. 'So you threw your wedding clothes into the rainwater?'

'Let's go to the kitchen.'

They found themselves in the kitchen. Mom was slicing onion to cook mutton.

'Mom, tell Papa everything in detail.' Ime returned to her room.

*

Papa stormed into Ime's room, the sword in his hand. It was their ancestral sword. Ime made sure Mom had told him everything, and, looking away from the shining blade of the sword, she gave attention to him to measure the volume of his anger likely to erupt into violence. She became so afraid she pulled him to a sit-down in the chair, unable to extricate the sword from his hand.

'Who are those two criminals, Ime? Tell me their names. I'll flood their houses with their blood right off. They can never escape from the charge of my sword. I'll never put down the sword until I quench its thirst with their blood. Just tell me their names, Ime.'

In the meantime, Mom entered the room and tried to extricate the sword from his hand.

'I couldn't identify them, Papa. They were wearing stocking masks. Now keep cool. I'll tell you their names if I can know them. I promise. Now pass the sword to Mom. She'll hand you the sword when time comes. We won't then prevent you from taking action.'

After Mom had taken the sword from his hand, he stood up, trying to recover his breath, unmindful of the sweat rolling down his face. 'What have they done to my sweet daughter? What have they done? They must quench the thirst of my sword. I'll find them out anyhow.' He started crying.

'Papa, don't cry. If you cry, I'll go mad.'

Putting the sword behind Ime's wardrobe, Mom sat by him and dried his tears with the end of her *chador*.

'Now I understand why you threw the wedding

clothes into the flood of rainwater. Tell the truth to Uddipan. He's a kind boy,' Papa said.

'Papa, he'll reject me.'

'I'll never give up. I'll again buy the same set of clothes for your wedding. If he rejects you, I'll sell our property and move to a new place. I'll find a suitable groom there. It's my duty.'

'I'll tell him the truth. But I'll never marry. I can't change my decision,' Ime said.

'We've distributed the wedding letters. Our preparation is almost over. Have you thought about these things? I don't know whose eyes have fallen on our family.' Mom looked towards the *namghar*. 'In the evening, I'll go to the *namghar* to light a *banti* and pray. Can you go with me, Ime?'

'Yes, I can. I'll also light a *banti* and pray.'

'Do I have to bring you more medicine?'

'The medicine has been very effective. The pain has almost seeped away.'

'You've quickly recovered. She guaranteed your quick recovery.'

Papa, who was silently listening to them, seemed as though he were deeply thinking of something. What was he thinking of? Was he thinking of Uddipan's rejection? Was he thinking of whether Uddipan would consider the situation? Was he thinking of how he'd move to a new place and what he'd do there? Was he thinking of structuring his future strategy? But he should never think of quenching the thirst of his sword.

When Papa went out with the sword from behind the

wardrobe, Mom said, 'If you tell Uddipan that you're a rape victim, he'll reject you.'

'On the foundations of lies you can't build a conjugal life.'

'That will be your blunder.'

'What'll happen if he knows the truth after my marriage? Can you imagine the consequences?'

'He'll never know it.'

'I'm sure the rapists snapped me. They'll blackmail me. They'll threat me with uploading them in the social media. They'll destroy my conjugal life.'

'Don't tell him the truth. It's my final advice.'

'Mom, I want to ask you two questions. Will you honestly answer the questions?'

'I want to first hear the questions.'

'Suppose I'm your son and the girl I'm engaged to is raped. Will you allow me to marry her? Suppose you don't know the rape. And the marriage is solemnized. What will you do when you happen to know it?'

'Don't tell him anything over the phone. Ask him to come to our house and then tell him the truth. I understand you won't change your decision.' Mom got up. 'Try to do it soon.'

18

Ime had called Uddipan several times. He hadn't received her calls. She'd sent him five messages at an interval of two minutes. In all the messages, she asked him to see her as soon as possible because there was something urgent, which she couldn't discuss over the phone. But he ignored the messages. Why did he ignore them? Did he do so adamantly or purposely? He shouldn't have done so. She didn't want to message him that she was a rape victim, though she could. She wanted to tell him everything, sitting face-to-face. His nonchalance increased her tension, and as a result of this, she couldn't help wriggling and wincing in the quagmire of the unfortunate situation and feeling the boredom that had begun since the time of her domestic captivity now assume a new dimension generating new apprehension to cramp her capabilities and compel her to wonder when her bad days would end or if they'd end at all. She'd feel better if she could go out like before, but her parents didn't allow her to go out.

'Try to feel better in the house. Your time to go out hasn't come yet, Ime,' Mom had said.

Now she was more worried about Pinto and Innes

than the rapists' sins and her wedding. Because Mom and Papa couldn't tell if they'd returned, she decided to know it from Pranati and called her.

'Have they come back home, Pranati?'

'No.'

'Did you receive any phone calls?'

'We're waiting for a phone call. Papa is ready to pay any amount of ransom.'

'Do you think they're kidnapped?'

'They just didn't return home from Guwahati. And that's all. They never remain out of contact. So we can't dismiss any possibilities.' Pranati sniffled.

Ime was almost on the verge of sniffling too. 'I'll call you later. Let's pray for the best.'

After the conversation, Ime went out to walk in the courtyard. While walking, she again mentally thanked Burha Bej's wife for the medicine, which had rapidly healed her pain and enabled her to walk like she used to. She remembered the novel she'd left on her table half-read was waiting to be finished. It was about a woman, rejected by society, and her subsequent struggles not to surrender to the male domination. The author made references to history and regretted through the voice of the protagonist that some men are too stupid to learn from history and act like civilized humans. She appreciated the subtle nuances under the layers of its deceptive simplicity. She disliked convoluted prose, so it was also one of the reasons why she appreciated the novel. Some modern writers in Assamese tended to write difficult novels and stories to perhaps set a modern trend. She avoided those stories because they taxed her brain. She thought those writers perhaps wrote to satisfy their egos and boast of contributing to real literary standards. She thought them to be just pretenders trying to set their individual standards, hungering for critical acclaim, and those writings were clusters of bushes where some critics enjoyed searching for pearls and finally relaxed with satisfaction. But the things they claimed as their new discoveries of new pearls to feel satisfied were just bits of some broken glass, and though not able to find the real pearls, they tried to flaunt their success they skipped no scope to boast of whenever a situation offered them opportunities. The engrossing thoughts that had meandered across her mind were necessary for her to forget her suffering and now to forget the reason why Pinto-da and Innes-bhai hadn't returned home. Like the books and magazines, such thoughts, necessary or unnecessary, right or wrong, helped her to escape from the hard reality that bore frustration to knock her into the lap of sorrow she imagined she would've been able to unburden at least to some extent if she could share it with Uddipan. The thoughts she'd tried to keep out might come back through that outlet and assume shapes of octopuses and render her inactive like they'd assumed the shapes several times in the past.

One day, she'd start writing the story of her pain and let the world define pain and realize its sharpness.

She turned to find herself in her room.

She sat down at her reading table, opened the novel to where she had put the bookmark, and started reading. She reached the climax. The light went out. Since the hailstorm, the electricity had become erratic. It was because of the wrong functioning of the transformer. From near the wardrobe, she brought the hurricane lamp to the table and went back to the novel, leaving the door partially open.

It took her about an hour to finish reading the novel.

Feeling thirsty and heaving a deep sigh, she stood up, went up to the filter in the corner of her room, poured her a glass of water, and drank it up, sitting on her heels. Then the second she was about to rise, she felt a hand touch her shoulder, thought it to be Mom's, and rose to her feet without looking back, and then as she turned her head to see Mom's face, the hand clutched her mouth — it clutched her mouth so tight she failed to even cry for help and realized she was in control of the image of a live fear, which in no time pushed her back to the edge of her bed.

'Who are you?' Ime asked, her heart thumping with fear.

'The witch. I've come down from the hills.' She sat on the plastic stool across from Ime. 'Don't shout. Just keep listening to me.'

Ime got frightened. What was the motive of the witch? Where was the old man now? Was the witch here to suck her blood and kill her to eat her heart? Fear benumbed her and, swallowing hard time and again, she couldn't wet her throat she'd wetted around more than two minutes ago.

'Why did you escape from the hills, without our permission? Did you think we wouldn't be able to find you?'

Too puzzled to answer the questions, for which she had answers, she kept sitting, not withdrawing her eyes from upon the witch. She was wearing a black maxi. Her face was covered with a piece of black cloth, and her hands were covered with black gloves, like in the hills. She could sense a note of violence in the witch's mood, though she couldn't see the witch's face.

'What are you thinking of? Just answer my questions, Ime. I hope you won't lie.'

Ime looked at the door.

'You can't go out, Ime.'

'I escaped from the hills because I was afraid of you and the old man.'

'Why were you afraid of us?'

'I saw you violently behave towards two persons tied to a tree.'

'They were our captives.'

'Why did you make them your captives? To suck their blood and eat their hearts?'

'They were criminals.'

'What were their crimes?'

The witch shifted on the stool. 'They were rapists.'

'How did you come to know they were rapists?'

'They raped you. They planned to make you a feast of jackals too. They would've made you a feast of jackals, if we hadn't rescued you.'

'What are their names?'

'Pinto Das and Innes Mullah.'

'They raped me? They wanted to make me a feast of jackals? I can't believe you. *I can't believe you.* Tell me you've come here to suck my blood and eat my heart. I can believe that. What's your real motive? If you don't go out right off, I'll call out to my parents.'

The witch reached into her bag, took out her pistol. 'If your parents come in, I'll simply kill them. So if you love your parents, don't call out to them.'

Ime, who felt like thrown into an oceanic hurricane, became speechless, her eyes fixed on her pistol, and wondered if she'd heard that voice elsewhere. She summoned up the courage.

'You didn't trust me, Ime.'

'You're a witch.'

'You didn't trust the old man either.'

'He was with you.'

The witch laughed a brittle laugh. 'The old man even couldn't think that you'd betray his trust. You violated his order.'

'How did I violate his order?'

'You ignored the boundary he'd made.'

'I was bound to do that.'

'Bound to do that?'

'Yes, bound to do that.'

'Why? Why bound to do that, Ime?'

'To escape from you.'

'Have you been able to really escape?'

'No,' Ime said. 'Would you tell me why you've come here?'

'Yes. I've come here to tell you about Pinto Das and Innes Mullah. They raped many girls. They raped and killed my daughter too. They tied me to a tree and set fire to my body. The old man happened to see the fire in the forest. He couldn't identify them because they escaped, just seeing him. They perhaps thought he was a cursed soul. He saved me. Then the two criminals set fire to our house.' The witch made a nasal sound. 'Now I live with him because I have no house to live in. I'm now too afraid to build a new house and live in it. The old man is very good. He is also a healer. He lives in the hills to practice medicine and black magic. He also lives in his cottage in the tea garden. People don't know he lives in the hills.'

Ime sat down, swallowed. 'Don't stop.'

'That fateful evening, my luck brought the old man to that area to hunt rabbit.'

'You should have returned to your home and filed a complaint with the police. Why didn't you file a complaint?'

'I understand I must produce proof.'

'Yes, I demand proof.' Ime suddenly became fearless. 'You may shoot me. You may do whatever you want to do to me. I don't fear you. Pinto-da can't be a rapist. He's my friend's brother. I love and respect him as my brother too.'

'I know he's Pranati's elder brother.'

'You know Pranati?'

The witch laughed, returned the pistol to her bag. 'I couldn't file a complaint because I couldn't identify them. I've identified them after making them our prisoners. If I'd been able to identify them before, I would've taken action against them myself.'

'Where's your husband now?'

'They killed him.'

'Why did they kill him?'

'Maybe because he identified them,' the witch said with sadness. 'Let me come to the real point.'

'Without producing proof, you shouldn't speak a single word against Pinto-da.'

'You should know the reason why they raped you.' The witch shifted on the stool. 'Pinto had a grudge against you. He wanted to marry you. When he happened to read your wedding letter, he became hopeless and angry.'

'Who told you about those things?'

'Our severe torture compelled them to admit to their crimes.' The witch took out a smart mobile from her bag. 'Come close to me and look at the proof.'

Ime obeyed. The witch switched on the mobile and opened the captured photos and Ime broke down to her knees with a shudder, just having a look at how they'd tied her hands and feet and how they'd committed sadistic violence on her, and then, unable to see her plundered and senseless naked body lying on the floor, she snatched the mobile from the witch's hand and switched it off. It was Pinto's smart mobile. Shocked by the revelation, no less excruciating than the rape, she lost her strength to stand up, tears coursing down her cheeks. The witch helped her to her feet and then to the bed.

'I have more proof.' The witch produced their stocking masks.

'Put them in the bag. You've shown me the actual proof. I don't want to see more proof.'

'My story is not finished yet.'

Ime looked at her fixedly.

'As usual, that evening too, we came out to hunt rabbit

in that area. A candle light drew our attention to that house. The old man was with me. We furtively went up to the house and saw you lying on the floor. They were drinking and talking in whispering voices. They were not wearing masks. We identified them. We had ropes with us. Ropes were for hunting purpose. We stormed into the house with our weapons. The sword was the old man's weapon. And the pistol was mine. I held the pistol at them. The old man tied their hands on their backs.' The witch slapped her knee to kill a mosquito. 'So, the old man first carried you to our den and then came back to help me. They tried to escape, but couldn't. Then we brought them to that place and tied them to the tree to make them a feast of jackals. We could shoot or pierce them with the sword. But we didn't do so. We wanted to kill them slowly. We wanted to make them feel suffering.' The witch swallowed. 'We brutally tortured them until midnight. Then we killed them with the sword and left them there so that they became a feast of jackals.'

'Where's their Scorpio?'

'The old man drove it to the gorge near the bridge at the beginning of the forest to the foot of the hills. It's still lying there with its wheels upward like a huge insect.'

'Are there so many jackals in the hills?'

The witch nodded.

'Where did you get this pistol?' Ime asked.

'Militants gave us this pistol. We helped them escape from police dragnet. When they became curious to know about us, I told them my story. They then gave us this pistol. They also gave us twelve rounds of bullets. For our protection. For taking revenge on them. And for doing justice.'

'Now I want to listen to *your* story.'

'You know my story.'

'I know your story?'

'Yes. You know my story. You know my story because you know me.'

'Tell me who you are. Tell me why you keep your face and hands covered. Now I must say you are not a witch.'

'Yes, I am not a witch. My name is Elmina Huro.'

'Mini's Mom? Joseph Uncle's wife Elmina Auntie?'

Auntie nodded.

'Your house was in the opposite side of the dry river. They set fire to your house on the night of June. We saw the fire leap up to the trees. That was a big fire.'

Auntie took the black cloth off her face, then the gloves off her hands. She then took off the maxi and stood in front of Ime in the lamplight. Ime shut her eyes. If she'd seen Auntie in the electric light, she would've been much more horrified. She thanked the power failure.

'Are you afraid to look at me, Ime?'

'Did Pinto Das and Innes Mullah really rape and kill Mini too?'

'Yes. They confessed.'

'She was my friend, Auntie.'

'I know.'

'Please put on your maxi and sit down.' Ime didn't look away from her.

Wearing the maxi, Auntie sat down. 'Garden Town and garden areas are now free from fear. They would've raped more girls if they'd been alive.' She looked back at the door. 'Luckily the old man saw the fire that night or I would've roamed the hills as a cursed soul at the moment.'

The light came on. Ime got frozen stiff with shock. Auntie immediately covered her face.

'They made my daughter a feast of jackals. Wasn't it justice to make them a feast of jackals?'

'The most appropriate justice.'

'We've left the hills. When the car will be found, the police will launch operation in the hills too. The illegal woodcutters often go by that place.'

'Why do you live in the hills?'

'You ask questions like my daughter. She was a good student. She wanted to be a teacher.'

'They raped me too, Auntie.'

'They would've also made you a feast of jackals if we hadn't rescued you from there.'

'You are my actual saviours. Now I understand.' She looked at Pinto's mobile. 'Auntie, will you give me the mobile?'

'What will you do with it?'

'I'll destroy it.'

'I'll destroy it myself. I'll drop it in a safe place. Even broken pieces hold clues. It must be carefully destroyed and discarded.'

'Okay.'

'I kept it with me as proof of their crime. To show you the proof.'

'May I get you another glass of water?'

She shook her head horizontally and got up.

'Auntie, can't you stay the night with us?'

'Thank you so much. I must go out of this place, in the cover of darkness. Now I'll go to the old man's cottage. The old man is waiting for me near the culvert. I've spent more time than I thought to spend.'

'How did you come here?'

'By an auto. It belongs to the son of the old man. The old man drove the auto.'

'Why didn't you bring him here?'

'He wanted to come. But I asked him to stay in the auto.'

'You've visited our house only to tell me how you've done justice?'

'Yes. And also to remove fear and anxieties from your mind.'

'Thank you so much, Auntie. Thank you so much!'

'Forget the bitter past and try to live happily. My blessing will remain with you forever. I'll always try to see my daughter in you.' Auntie touched Ime's head and went out with her bag.

Ime decided to first tell her parents about Auntie's visit, the two rapists, and the justice done to them, and then go to the old man's cottage to give him thanks and seek his forgiveness.

19

The next morning, unable to contain what Elmina Huro had told her, Ime found Papa and Mom in the kitchen. Then just after Ime had elaborated on how she'd happened to learn from Elmina Huro how Pinto Das and Innes Mullah had raped her and what had happened to Mini, Papa threw the cigarette from between his fingers, rushed into his room, and came out with the sword, hidden in a gunnysack under his cot.

'Now they can't escape my sword. I'll ruin their families. I won't rest until I redden the blade of my sword with their blood.'

Mom quickly grasped Papa's hand and obstructed him with her outstretched hands. 'I've always thought Pinto as a good boy. Now our wisdom is to forget the past and give attention to the wedding. Not shouting for revenge. The criminals had been properly punished.' Mom released the sword from his hand.

'Don't think of my wedding, Mom. I'll tell him the truth. My physical pain has drained away. But my mental pain won't drain away until I tell him the truth. I can never forget I'm a rape victim,' Ime said when Papa sat on the side of the veranda, looking at her face.

'Your Papa again bought the same set of wedding clothes. So you must alter your decision.'

'I can't cheat him.'

'Parents think the best for their children,' Papa said.

Whenever Ime would feel disconcerted, she would take her album from the wardrobe and open it, and now, coming to her room, as she took her album and opened it, her eyes sat fixedly on Uddipan's photos. 'Will you be able to stand the news of my rape, Uddipan? You can't. I know you can't. But I must tell you the truth and ask you to treat the wedding as cancelled. For that I must detach myself from my thought of you,' she said to the photo, in which he was standing close to his bike. Resolved to tell him about the incident right now, she lifted the mobile and the question whether she was going to do right or wrong appeared in front of her eyes, like a massive pillar; her hands shivering, she immediately put down the mobile, stood by the window, and thoughtfully looked out at the rose plant. She'd nurtured it like her dream and it'd stood as a symbol of their love since the afternoon when she and Uddipan had planted it. Though she wished to go out and uproot it right off to demolish all her dreams, a good sense caught her mind and in seconds prompted her to realize that the plant was not responsible for the cancellation of the wedding, and she immediately transferred her mind to her fate, from the nastiness of cruelty to the plant. The old man and Auntie shouldn't have rescued her or she shouldn't have returned home from the hills. It would've been better if she'd taken a wrong direction into the deep forest and got lost. She looked at her mobile again. 'I must call him. I must tell him the truth right this moment,' she said to the rose plant and got ready to call him, the throat feeling like getting blocked.

Mom came in. 'Did you talk to Uddipan?'

'Leave me to myself, Mom.'

'Everything now depends on Uddipan.'

'Do you think Uddipan will accept me even after knowing that?'

'Uddipan is a very good boy. And innocent too.'

'Can the wife of Burha Bej find a solution to my problem?'

'She is not a healer of mental wounds.'

'I feel scared. I can't live if he leaves me. I love him so much, Mom. He also loves me like I love him.'

'We can't wait. The wedding day is almost near at hand.'

'I'm afraid of his reaction. I'm afraid he can't stand the blow.'

'Ask him to come to our house. Sit together and discuss the matter.'

Given the present situation that was partially in her favour because the criminals were no more in the world, she thought she required to sit alone, undisturbed, to thoroughly brood over what she was going to do, and for doing so, she couldn't think of any other suitable places than under the *kolajam* tree, where she eventually went, the mobile in her hand, and seated herself in the chair. As she got ready to punch his number, she felt her fingers freeze. She could hide the fact to marry him. But she couldn't dismiss the fact that it'd be an act of injustice to his confidence in her chastity. A raped girl is often compelled to spend her life like a raped girl. The pus a rapist pours into his victim pollutes the victim's entire life. Now she was such a victim, and, being such a victim, she could never sin to hide the fact to marry him. LOVE was still vivid in dark dots in the valley of her breasts. Marks hadn't totally disappeared from her cheeks despite the regular use of Boroline. At present she could manage to lie to him and hide her stain. But in the future? It couldn't be guaranteed that the fact would never come to light in the future. And if it happened to come to light, the consequences would never be in her favour. So it was her right decision to tell him the truth and give up the thought of marriage forever. He was her love. He was next to her heart. He'd remain so forever. Papa's decision to leave Garden Town was a right decision. But, even after settling in a new place, she wouldn't help but live her cursed life. She stopped thinking and rose from the chair to go to her room, disgruntled at her inability to call Uddipan.

She read *LOVE.*

20

Uddipan called her and Ime decided to receive his call and tell him the truth. But, after looking at the mobile that made her more nervous than before, she got off and sat on the stool Huro Auntie had sat on and kept sitting until she felt compelled to walk out of the suffocating atmosphere of the room to breathe in the cool breeze blowing across the courtyard. It was midnight. The moon had come out in the clear sky sprinkled with stars. She casually looked up at the flying bats and listened to the soothing rhythms of drums wafting from a garden. The tea garden people were perhaps drinking and dancing.

She walked into the garden and stood under the *amla* (Indian gooseberry) tree Ata had planted and she'd stood many times with Uddipan under. The rose bush Uddipan had planted in her garden was now better than before. The other plants were also rising vibrantly. Now they didn't look affected by the hailstorm. Coming to their house, he used to pluck a flower from that rose plant and offer it to her. Before long, the plant would be in bud and invite butterflies. While thinking like that, she couldn't help but think he would never come to their house to see the flowers and pluck one to offer her as in the past after being aware of the crime against her virginity. She could never imagine living without him. He was next to her heart. He was her heart beat. He was so gentle, so considerate, and so kind. He was for her; she was for him. Whenever he had come to Garden Town from Guwahati to visit his Uncle, he had visited her, and he had never tried to do anything bad to her. His amorous access had remained limited only to her back, her hands, her long hair, and their hugs and kisses. His chest was wide, and she could feel his muscles as she'd laid her hand on him. He was five feet six inches—three inches taller than her. He had Levis jeans and denim jacket on when she'd first seen him. He was a nice man and his niceness was as appealing to her as his handsomeness. Would he accept her when she'd tell him the details of what had happened to her? Was there a man with so large a heart full of kindness? He thought her to be an honest and innocent girl. How could she tell him that she was raped? And she couldn't lie to destroy the life of an honest young man with beautiful dreams of a beautiful family with beautiful wife and children. Her love for him was not temporary. She'd wished to live for him and for his children forever. He was really very handsome, very polite, very brilliant. None ever criticized him. Girls vied to talk to him, to listen to his poems, to be close to his heart. If the rapists had made her a feast of jackals, she would've been really fortunate. The family members along with the rape victim suffer the stain. With many efforts, she'd taken the hard decision. Though it was against her mind, she'd been constrained to take it because no other options had been left for her, and for that reason she had to weep a lot. She anomalously recalled the same things and same questions and wondered if that was a sign of the beginning of insanity, and next moment, when she racked her brain to find the reason why she should go insane and failed to find any, she laughed off her stupidity causing the cobweb of her thoughts and determined to try to forget her past and control her anomalous emotions so she didn't feel like going insane.

She came back to her room and called Uddipan.

He received her call at the sixth ring. 'Hello,' he said in a sleepy voice. 'Is anything wrong with you, Ime?'

'Why this question, Uddipan?'

'Try to answer this question yourself. May I not want to know if there is something wrong if you constantly ignore my calls? Read the time. It's 1:56 am. Are you okay? Are your parents okay?'

'Everything okay, Uddipan. Everyone okay.'

'Feel free to tell me if you have any problem.'

'No problem.'

'We've almost finished distributing our letters. Hope you've also distributed your letters.'

Though she thought that was the right moment to tell him the truth, she didn't have the strength.

'Hello, Ime. Are you lost in something?'

'I'm lost in thoughts.'

'What thoughts?'

'Thoughts of you.'

'Thoughts of me? Good.' He laughed and kissed aloud. 'I can't stay without you, Ime. I'm just waiting for May 26. Now the days and nights have become so long for me. Have they also become so for you?'

'I'll talk to you a lot when we meet. So come to our house soon.'

'Try to receive my calls. Your dulcet voice gets me to feel you beside me, Ime. I always want to hear your voice.' He gently coughed. 'I'm so busy with the preparation for the wedding. Papa, who has now stood corrected, has given me the full responsibility.'

'Please do find time to visit me soon. I have to discuss an important matter with you.'

'Can you drop a hint?'

'You'll know when you visit me. So visit me soon without fail.'

'I'll try.'

'Good night.'

'Good night. Have a sweet dream.'

Sweet dream? That fateful night she'd lost her dream. Those two criminals had crushed her dream like the rain tree had crushed their grocery shop. Uddipan's voice in her ears, she got into bed, and being sure of his visit, though she lay down and tried to sleep, trying to banish all those thoughts from her mind, she failed to do so because his face prominently appeared in her mind and made her roll from side to side, and then, as she felt her throat dry, she got out of bed and drank the glass of water she'd kept on the table. The water cooled her throat, but not her mind and she felt so agitated her mind went to Gauhati University where she'd planned to read and he'd also inspired her to read after marriage, his mother and sister supporting his views to their pleasure. Since Garden Town had become cursed for them, they must leave it and go to a new place and live like in a hideout away from all known people, including Uddipan, his parents, sister, and uncle, and all as well. She'd never forget him. She wouldn't be able to forget him. With her, she'd preserve the album and open it when her mind wept for him. She again tried to sleep. But as she realized it was difficult to sleep, she got up, opened a window, and stood by it, absorbed in the decadence of her anomalous thoughts, and then after around five minutes, she heard her mobile ring and left the window to pick it up—the call from Uddipan.

'Are you still awake, Ime? What are you doing?'

'I'm standing by the window and watching the rose buds in the plant you planted.' She smiled towards the buds she could now see in the street light. 'May I know what you are doing?'

'I'm reading a newspaper.'

'Is it time to read a newspaper, Uddipan?'

'If it's time to watch rose buds, it can be time to read a newspaper.' He loudly smacked his lips. 'Actually, I'm too busy to find time to read even a newspaper in daytime.'

'Go to bed.' She closed the window noisily. 'I'm going to bed.'

'Did you read yesterday's edition of the *Agradoot*?'

'No. Any good news?'

'A twelve-year-old girl was gang-raped and dropped beside a road,' he said. 'Never go out alone.'

She licked her lips. She was lost for words. She started walking from one side of the room to another one.

'Hello, hello Ime.'

'I feel sorry for the unfortunate girl.'

'Go to bed and have sweet dreams about your future life.'

'I feel sorry for the rape victim.'

'Your voice has changed all of a sudden. You've become emotional. Don't hide anything from me, Ime. Please don't try to hide anything from your would-be husband.'

'I feel upset about the unlucky girl.'

'I'll never give you such news in the future. I'm sorry for disturbing your mind. I'm going to bed. Hope you're also going to bed. I'll talk to you in the morning. Receive my call like this. Now sleep well. I won't let you sleep after May 26.' He laughed and kissed audibly.

'Thank you.'

Putting down the mobile, she turned to the mirror and touched her cheeks, her chest heaving. She'd felt comfortable about talking to him and listening to his sonorous voice. The talk had lessened her aloneness to a little extent. It would've been better if he hadn't told her about the news of the twelve-year-old rape victim. As she thought to withdraw from the mirror, she saw the mirror mock at her nervousness and then, not moving from where she was standing, facing the mirror, she again determined to collect the courage and strength and to survive the rape, since she was aware that backing from her determination would expel her into the abyss of darkness she was too afraid to even think of. She swallowed hard. Her worries would perhaps end only after they moved to a new place. She ran her fingertips over her left cheek. She heard Papa cough in his room. Doubtful about that he was sleeping, she thoughtfully sat at her table, her chin in the cups of her upright hands resting on it. She didn't know how long this crime against women would continue, if that would continue until the existence of the last woman in the world. People wrote articles about the rape victims with anger and sympathy, and the government made loud promises to take stern measures to control the crime. She had no nerve to dismiss those articles as something useless. It wasn't possible for the government to guard every person. She stood up and started walking in the room. For self-defence, the women must learn martial art. She was sure he'd reject her. But, fearing the rejection, she'd never cancel her determination. As she thought he'd find a beautiful girl if he left her, a flow of jealousy that began to meander through her mind compelled her to wonder if it was right to be jealous of an imaginary girl and if it became her. Except her breaths nothing was now audible in her room, and her mind was so disturbed she couldn't think of anything coherently and felt to be on the verge of losing her logic. She breathed a deep sigh, went to bed. She needed a deep sleep.

21

Ime was wiping her face after breakfast. She heard her phone ring. She hurried into her room to pick up the phone. 'Good morning, Uddipan.'

'Good morning, my chaste beauty!'

'I suppose you're coming to our house.'

'I'll come in time.' He gently grunted. 'May I put down the phone to talk to the confectioner? He'll supply sweets for the wedding.'

'Okay.' She put down the mobile.

The memory of the rape now returned with all the bitterness that it had and gave her more nervousness than it'd given and she almost lost her balance and wanted to fly to his place, and by the time she realized the reality of her ability, she called him. But he didn't take her call, and not stopping calling him continuously, she finally felt forced to give up, thinking he was maybe still talking to the confectioner. Within a few seconds after she hung up, he called her and before exchanging pleasantries in a frivolous way, it was his habit, regretted being unable to receive her call. As he steered the conversation to impractical things, she wanted to cut the conversation because of the situation she was in. But, instead of discouraging him, she let the conversation continue, acting the role of a passive listener and choosing to limit her response to just nasal monosyllables. She got he was in a mood to roam another territory to prolong the conversation and asked him to come to their house soon. He told her to drop a hint, despite her repeating that she wouldn't tell him unless they sat together. After he'd promised to visit her as soon as possible, she hopefully put down the phone and took his photo from under the pillows and touched it to her lips, kissing like not kissing, before steadying her look on the cut mark on his left cheek. The mark made him cuter and sexier. Though it was a thin mark, her attention made it prominent at present. She'd first kiss the mark and caress it with her fingers and lips when he'd be hers. Her mood suddenly changed and the room felt airless, and to breathe in fresh air, she came out and sat under the *kolajam* tree, and then, looking at the sun above the shoulders of the hills, she tried to withhold the flow of her thoughts and emotions with a view to feeling relaxed.

Uddipan called her again. Annoyed and anxious, she answered the call and wanted to know if he was coming within a day or two.

But not telling her anything about that, he said abruptly, 'The malady of rape is spreading like an epidemic in our society. I sympathise with the rape victims. My heart weeps for them. I fear the rapists. I have a beautiful fiancée at Garden Town. It's not a secure place at all. I have a beautiful sister in Guwahati. You can't say Guwahati is a secure place either.' He sucked his teeth. 'The women are very insecure nowadays.'

'Who is responsible for this insecurity?'

'Everybody is responsible for this insecurity. Our families are responsible. Our society is responsible. Our government is responsible. Our women are responsible. Our men are responsible. Our technologies are responsible. I can mention more and more. So everybody is responsible. None can make a getaway.'

'You've generalized the responsibility. The women were raped before the use of technologies too.'

'Right. More than one lakh women were kidnapped and raped during the Partition. During the riots, innumerable women became rape victims. Rape is a tool a man uses to satisfy his masculine urge. This is male chauvinism. Rapists are sadists, perverts. Every rape victim has revealed this fact.'

'You never talked like that, Uddipan. You never sounded so worried.'

'Whenever you open a newspaper, you'll find at least one report on rape.'

'I skip those pages.'

'You can skip those pages. But can you ...?'

'You really never talked like that, Uddipan. What has happened to you? You read newspapers before too.'

'Nothing has happened to me. Nothing can happen to me as long as you're with me. I talk like this because my heart melts with sympathy for a rape victim, who is always one hundred per cent innocent.' He paused for a few moments. 'It has become a huge problem in our country. Since 2010 this crime has increased by 7.1 per cent. Our country ranks third for the number of the registered rape cases. Do you know how many women were raped in our country in 2012?'

'No.'

'Around 24, 923. Maybe more than this. You can't get the data of the unreported cases. From a seven-year-old girl to a seventy-year-old woman, none is secure from a rapist. Even a nun is targeted by a rapist.' He sneezed. 'I thought US women are safer than Indian women. My thinking was wrong. The US ranks first for the number of rape cases. A woman is raped every 20 minutes in India. On the contrary, every 6.2 minutes a woman is raped in the United States. In India, almost 77% rapists go acquitted. If the parents of the victims are poor, they can't fight a legal battle against the rapists. In the United States and in other western countries, the rape victims are treated better than in India.' He noisily sucked his teeth. 'Women must learn martial arts for their self-defence. Only writing newspaper articles and books, you cannot do anything. Rapists cannot be controlled by pens. For safety reason you cannot remain confined within. For safety reason you cannot stay without responding to your various responsibilities.'

She wondered if he'd listened to Pinto's speech in the football field that afternoon and remained silent for a few seconds before saying, 'Will you talk more?'

'Majority of the rape victims are in the 18-30 age groups. In India, rape victims are considered unfit for marriage. The rape victims often become burden to their families. Like them their families suffer ostracism.'

She was 22 years and 5 months old when she was raped. *In India, rape victims are considered unfit for marriage.* As she mentally repeated the line, she felt like falling down.

'Aren't you listening, Ime?'

'You've talked a lot. Now please find time to see me as soon as possible. I must tell you something.'

'You can tell me right this moment too.'

'I'll tell you only when you come to our house.'

'Then keep waiting for my visit.'

'The sooner, the better for me.'

He called her twice after she had put down the mobile. Not taking the call, she sat on the side of her bed and looked out of the window at her small sky, and whenever she looked at the sky through that window, she sometimes became thoughtless and sometimes so thoughtful she felt her eyes stuck to the small sky, like glue, which continued until the strain forced tears to course down her cheeks. Why did he talk about rape like that? The talk doubled her tension. If he hadn't talked about rape like that, she wouldn't have got so tensed up. Why did he talk like that? Was it because he felt concerned about her security? Maybe. It was natural. Only a lucky girl would be his wife. But she wasn't lucky at all. *In India, rape victims are considered unfit for marriage.* Her mind didn't allow her to accept that just as a general perception without a specific meaning none but her could sense the best at the moment, and she felt her tension increase when the thought that she was unfit to become his wife and her dream would remain unfulfilled forever occupied her mind. Resolute to never cheat Uddipan, she'd already boldly prepared herself to live an ostracised life, following the dictates of destiny. She pulled herself from the forest of her thoughts and turned to stare at Mom when Mom wandered into the room and wanted to know if she was talking to Uddipan or someone else. Ime wasn't in a mood to talk, and so, Mom went out after instructing Ime not to get herself in a dither over telling Uddipan the reason so that their behaviour couldn't be interpreted as an unpardonable offence.

Papa had already planned to sell the properties and move to a place where none would know them except their close relatives. She ran her fingers over her cheeks. The marks were still faintly visible. She stood by the window and looked out. The garden was in bloom. Desiring to spend time with the flowers, she went out to the garden and stood under the *amla* tree. She picked a dry twig from under the tree and played with it for a while before throwing it towards a butterfly. It didn't hit the butterfly, and the butterfly, which, to her, indicated the stability of her love and gave her happiness and confidence, flew off the flower after sometime, and she lovingly touched the flower it'd spent time with. She started walking in the garden, tenderly touching the flowers, not giving importance to the goat trying to enter the garden and then going back with failure. The people, who went along the street, looked in her direction, and though some of them were known to her, she tactfully avoided their eyes and they didn't feel inspired to talk to her. The butterflies moved, undisturbed. Before leaving Garden Town, she thought to do the shopping because they would never come back after they left the town.

She felt sad.

22

Two mornings later, Uddipan answered her call in such a harsh voice that it set her heart racing and made her put down the phone and sit motionless, not able to find words to call him again and speak. Mounting tension scorching her inside, she felt so thirsty she wished to drink the entire water from her filter, and drinking two glassfuls of water, as she nervously stood by the window, she felt her eyes settle on the street, empty of everything but dust and gravel. She wouldn't have looked away from the dust and gravel if the mobile hadn't rung again and forced her to answer the call.

'When are you exactly coming to our house, Uddipan?'

'Why are you repeating the question? Why don't you tell me if there is something wrong?'

'I can't tell you that over the phone. How many times should I repeat it?'

'You sound worried about something. I'm sure you're worried about something or you're trying to hide something from me. Am I right? If I'm right I'd ask you not to even try to hide anything from me. You are my would-be *wife* and I am your would-be *husband*. While talking to you, I've sensed fear in your voice. Are you afraid of me?'

'You can't know anything unless you come.'

'Fear or lie is an open sword between the spouses. Remember it forever if you want to live a happy conjugal life.'

'Tell me exactly when you're coming.'

'You're extremely worried about something. I'll come as soon as possible. Only a few letters are to be distributed. Just let me finish distributing the letters.' He laughed. 'I'm sure you'll look like a princess at the wedding.'

'Ime is a daughter of a poor paper distributor and grocer.' She ran her fingers over her cheeks. 'You must come tomorrow. If you fail to do so, you can't find me anywhere. Now I'll charge my mobile.'

'Okay.'

After the mobile had been plugged in, she carried the kettle of hot water into the bathroom and put it near the bucket full of cool water. Taking cool water in a mug from the bucket, she poured water on her head. Then, puffing out her cheeks, she sprayed another mug of water on her closed eyes. The eyes felt cool. She sprayed more water, and then she mixed the hot water with the cool water of the bucket to make the water as warm as she needed. She thoroughly soaped her body and took a long bath. Feeling fresh and energetic, she emerged from the bathroom and spread her clothes on the clothesline in the courtyard before coming into her room to dry her hair in front of the mirror. She combed her hair into a parting in the middle and minutely studied her face.

She unplugged the mobile, and Uddipan came to her thought again and unwilling to call him, she found herself in the garden, the only place to forget the cause for the agitation of her mind, which was now too agitated to be in control. Her head down, she began to walk, silently talking to the flowers and sincerely expecting to see a butterfly. Deep concentration on the garden helped her cool her mind a little bit, and she continued walking, not raising her head even when she heard people go by except when she saw Papa come back after distributing papers.

Suddenly, the horn of a bike in front of the gate broke her concentration and she turned her head back and seeing Uddipan gracefully get off his bike, she stood motionless, wondering where he was at the time of her talking to him since it wasn't possible for him to come from Guwahati so soon and because of that there was every possibility of his being at his Uncle's, and stopping wondering about those matters she now thought less important than readying her mind to enter into the crucial discussion she'd repeatedly asked him to come for, she walked ahead with calculated steps to open the gate to welcome him so that he could come in and as usual keep his bike at the concrete strip through the garden. 'I'm happy you've come, Uddipan,' she said, a smile crossing her lips. His eyes smiling up at her face, as he put his right hand on her shoulder, she made sure the signs of worries on her face had gone unnoticed. The worries had come from the thought that she wouldn't be able to address him with an effusion of love anymore in the future, after revealing the fact to him. 'Why are you looking at me like this? Have you seen me for the first time?' She swallowed. 'Let's go in.'

'Thank you. I'm in a hurry. I've come with a special purpose.'

When they sat under the *kolajam* tree, Papa found himself in the chair next to Uddipan and enquired about Uddipan's parents and their wedding preparations. Then after talking about this and that, Papa wanted to know if he'd spent the night at his Uncle's or come directly from Guwahati, and she listened to Uddipan's answer satisfying her curiosity. He had come to Garden Town a week ago to invite some people to his wedding.

As Papa went away, Uddipan pointed to the hills with his brows. 'I want to spend some time with you at our favourite rendezvous.'

'At the bridge?'

'Yeah.'

She immediately thought that a chance and said in English, 'Your pleasure is my pleasure.'

23

With Ime riding pillion, Uddipan drove his bike slowly and not going towards the bridge, when he turned left and she wanted to know where he was going, he didn't answer. He took the dirt road snaking up towards the forest in the hills east of where the cursed hills were. She pressured him to tell her about the exact destination he was stubbornly taking her to.

'Just keep sitting, silently enjoying the surroundings,' he said aloud, sounding irritated.

Now having nothing in her mind except her decision and tension, she chose to keep sitting silently and breathe deeply to feel relaxed, not disturbing him with her questions about his purpose and the destination.

*

After an hour, Uddipan stopped at the beginning of the plain. 'We've reached our destination.'

Following him, she got off. Riding high up was enjoyable. She looked back at the distance they'd crossed and then at the sea of green under the ascending sun, at the plain dotted with small houses comprising a small village, at men, women, and their children here and there, and at the grazing cattle before exchanging smiles with the children who came up to the bike, for chocolates from him.

'Let's go ahead.' He began to walk.

'Why have we come here, Uddipan?'

'Robin Rabha lives in this village. He is one of my friends. I've come here to invite him to my wedding. He's the only man we're going to invite together.'

'If I'd guessed your intention, I wouldn't have accompanied you. I asked you to visit me so I could tell you a secret. You said you'd take me to the rendezvous at that bridge. I must tell you something very urgent and important.'

'If you don't want me to invite my friend because he lives in such a village, I won't.'

'I won't marry you. I can't marry you.'

'Then I won't invite this friend. Hope you'll then marry me.' He laughed out loud.

'No, that's not the cause.'

'Then what's the cause?' He stared into her face. 'Let's go to the bank of the lake.' He started walking towards the lake, her hand in his.

They got to the bank and sat down. He pointed his index finger at a pair of Saras cranes, which were diving and coming out of water. Every time they came out, they shook their heads, unmindful of other birds. The clusters of water lily were in bloom. There were insects on the floating leaves of the water lily. The insects, which flew above the flowers and the leaves, sat on the leaves before flying off. The fish agitated the water. A kingfisher swooped down on a fish and went back to its position on the branch of a small tree leaning down to the cluster of pink water lily. The sun was now above their heads and the shade of the tree they were silently sitting under didn't fall into the water. It was a tree with new leaves. Like she'd enjoyed taking in the beauty of the forest while riding pillion, she now enjoyed taking in the pleasant view: it was a sea of green; the forest around the village silently boasted of belonging to the series of small hills skirting the lake to their west. At the time of starting out on the road into the hills, she couldn't imagine having a view of such a nice lake. Through the silence between them, she observed that he was still absorbed in the details of the lake alive with the pair of Saras cranes playing as before.

'Uddipan, did you inform your friend about our arrival?'

'You didn't answer my question.'

Though unwilling to hurt him, now she thought she couldn't help doing so and gathered the courage to answer his question, for building her conjugal life on the foundations of a stain was beyond her imagination. 'I've decided not to marry you because of a stain,' she said, her heart pounding.

'Because of a stain? What stain?'

'It is not an ordinary stain, Uddipan. It is a stain of rape. They raped me. Now I am not your Ime anymore. I am a rape victim.' She failed to fight off her tears.

His lips pressed tight and his stare piercing right through her face, he nodded his head before resting his hands on his upright knees, and then as he put his head on the bridge of his hands, she touched the veins on the backs of his hands and he looked up, his lips quivering, no words coming out, and his anger slowly melting into tears to get stuck to his stubble, like dew on blades of grass. He straightened himself. His face muscles loosened. Calm settled on his face. She didn't ask him why he'd grown stubble though she wanted.

'Were you responsible for the rape? Did you invite Pinto Das and Innes Mullah to rape you? You are not guilty of that.' He threw a stone into the lake. 'Forget the rapists forever. Only remember Burha Bej and Elmina Huro and their justice.'

'How did you know it?'

'I listened at your window while Elmina Huro was talking to you. For more details, I then met her at Burha Bej's house in the same night. Burha Bej is still angry with you. I'll take you to him. You should seek his pardon.'

'Yes, I must do it before we leave Garden Town.'

'I don't understand.'

'We can't live at Garden Town anymore with the stain.'

'Where will you go?'

'To a new place. To live with new people.'

'So because of the rape the wedding is cancelled?'

'*In India, rape victims are considered unfit for marriage.*'

'That's a general perception.'

'Has your Papa changed his mind?'

'He'll be a loving Papa in your presence.'

When a child blew the horn of his bike, he looked back and the child kept standing, smiling towards them.

'Are you angry, Uddipan?'

'Mom poured icy water on Papa's anger. Now he's on good terms with me.'

'Not the answer to my question.'

'Look at the clusters of water lily. Look at the flowers. You like pink flowers or white flowers?'

'Both pink and white,' she said, gazing at the pink flowers.

'I must say you like pink flowers more than white ones. All flowers are immaculate.'

She nodded. 'Are you angry with me?'

Not saying anything, he went down to the edge of water, plucked a pink flower, and then, coming back to where she was, he cast an admiring look at the flower and went up to his bike. He looked at her over his shoulder, opened the tool box, and took out a wedding letter. He came back and sat beside her. 'This is the last wedding letter to be distributed.' He held out the letter to her, the flower in his left hand. 'We'll give this letter together to my friend.' He rested his chin on her shoulder. 'I'll remain beside you as long as I live. Now none can even dare to touch your hair.' He raised his head. 'Look at the pair of Saras cranes. From now on we'll live like this pair and dive and swim in the lake of our love. You're still as immaculate as this water lily, Ime.'

Her tongue stuck in the palate, her heart rapidly palpitating, and the frequency of her irregular breathing increasing, she burst into tears, feeling lifted to the crest of a hill.

'Smile, Ime, smile and promise to keep smiling forever like a water lily in the lake of my love.' He presented her with the lily, wiped her cheeks, and pulled her into his bosom.

She looked into his eyes through her tears, before starting rubbing her nose against his chest, not caring the two children watching them. 'I'll smile. I promise I'll keep smiling like a water lily in the lake of your love,' she said, her eyes flitting between the water lily in her hand and the lake.

'Let's go. I'll have to go back to Guwahati before evening.' He got up.

The flower in her hand and the letter in his, they walked towards the house of his friend, the two children following them. She looked back at the children, her eyes shining with happiness.

'May I recite the poem I wrote to recite to you?' He put his left hand on her right shoulder.

She tilted her head right.

'Listen.'

i live the life to live with you

my life is a slipstream of your life

the dust on my life is your grace i'll never dust

i'd better live in your dustbin

than on my bed of rose

like your slipstream let me live

'Did you really write it for me?'

'Trust me.'

'I love and trust you at the same time, Uddipan.'

Black Eagle Books

www.blackeaglebooks.org
info@blackeaglebooks.org

Black Eagle Books, an independent publisher, was founded
as a nonprofit organization in April, 2019. It is our mission
to connect and engage the Indian diaspora and the world at
large with the best of works of world literature published on
a collaborative platform, with special emphasis on
foregrounding Contemporary Classics and New Writing.